A TIDE SO Dark

A World of Ausher Novella

EMBER DRAKE

The future will
be painted in
blood and ink.

A TIDE SO Dark

A WORLD OF AUSHER NOVELLA

EMBER DRAKE

Content/Trigger Warning

Warnings for A Tide So Dark contain intense and potentially upsetting themes, including:

- ❖ Violence
- ❖ Sexual assault
- ❖ Explicit sexual content

CHAPTER I

T he wind blew gently through her long black tresses as she watched them through the window, hidden in the evening shadow. A soft smile touched her lips. He looked well and happy, her dragon. She did not think he would ever find love considering how he grew up, but here he was building a simple life with his lover. In a bookstore of all places. With a contented sigh, she moved away from the shop and went on with her evening.

She hummed as she leisurely strolled down the street, smiling as she passed the street sign that said Pirates Alley. It was a fitting place for his new life, with a small reminder of his old one. She wanted to go in and speak to him but decided not to. It would not do him well to see her again after all the time that had passed since they last saw each other. They did not part ways on the best of terms, but she still wished him well. After all that he had been through—all that she had put him through—he deserved some peace.

As she continued to walk, passing people and listening as the sounds of jazz filled the night, she got the distinct feeling that she was being followed. It was nothing out of the ordinary for her. She was half succubus and half vampire—a dhampir—and it brought her a wealth of attention. Though sometimes, like tonight, it was unwanted.

She was content to spend her evening alone, but her pursuer's scent was strong. He smelled of decay and the sea, and it was somewhat familiar. She had smelled it before when she first arrived in the city, but thought nothing of it then.

Hoping to lose her tail, she merged with a group admiring a street performer. After some time had passed and she no longer smelled his scent, she moved on. She made her way past Jackson Square, and there it was again. The smell of the sea and death. She quickly got through the crowd and ducked down an alley. Pulling her daggers from inside her coat, she readied herself for a confrontation. Shortly after she went into the alley, the stranger that followed appeared at the entrance, his face hidden under a dark hood.

"Lovely evening for a stroll, don't ya think?" she asked, her grip on her daggers tight.

"Indeed, it is," he replied, his voice sounding gnarled and distorted. "It's been a long time, Ivy Thatch."

She narrowed her eyes at him. "I see you've heard of me."

"Heard of you? No, I made you."

"If I had a penny for every time I heard that from a man," she laughed. "Come on, then," she started after a moment. "Show me that pretty face."

2

Slowly, he removed the hood of his cloak, revealing long, dark hair that framed cold, ice-blue eyes in a pale face she had not seen in over two hundred years.

She sucked in air sharply, taking a step back. "No," she whispered. "It can't be you. You're dead."

He grinned broadly. "Yes, it would seem that it didn't take."

"How?" she growled, pointing at the nasty scar that sat on the left side of his neck and traveled down his collarbone and shoulder with her blade. "Andr venom is lethal."

"That's the thing about water elementals and poisons. Perhaps it wasn't wise to throw me into the sea," he explained, his hands splayed out at his sides.

"Then I'll finish what he started!" she roared as she lunged forward, but her movements were halted.

Her daggers clattered to the ground as she fought to break his hold. He summoned her to him by an invisible force, the toes of her boots dragging against the street while she continued to struggle. She bared her fangs as she came face to face with her greatest demon.

"I really must thank you for finding my dragon for me," he smiled, roughly cupping her face. "He has been very difficult to track down after his time with that circus."

"You can't kill him; he's immortal," she said through gritted teeth.

He got in close, pressing his cheek against hers, and whispered in her ear, "Who said I wanted to kill him? Why kill him when I can break his new toy?"

Her eyes went wide when she realized what he meant. "You can't," she gasped.

"Oh, but I will. And he will watch," he purred. "But you won't be around to enjoy the show."

Ivy felt a tear roll down her cheek before it crystalized and shattered on the ground. She felt the blood in her veins thicken and slow, turning cold. Freezing. She watched

3

helplessly as he stepped back, then his hand made a tight fist. As her organs shut down, her heart stopping, she took one last breath as the darkness enveloped her. The last thing she saw was his smiling, demonic face before there was nothing.

CHAPTER 2

T he wooden sign that read *Bound to Please* creaked in the breeze, the edges occasionally crackled with faint electric sparks. Inside the shop, the air was tense. A regular customer, and a regular annoyance, harassed the owners.

"Really, dear, why do you always dress like a man?" squawked the old woman. "People will get the wrong impression of you."

Korlue rolled his eyes and sighed in exasperation as he held onto his snarling mate. The old woman, Madam Delphine, was an obnoxious old broad with bad eyes who always assumed Korlue was a woman dressed as a man. No matter how many times she had been corrected.

"People are free to think what they want, but I am a man, Madame Delphine," he said, barely calming Andrew down as Madame Delphine clutched her pearls in response to the aggression. "Was there anything in particular that you wanted today?"

Madame Delphine was a local mystic who frequented the shop, sometimes bringing chaos with her. Like the time she came into the store with a storm spirit sealed in an old book. She was a miserable old crone with nothing better to do.

"You poor, sweet, delusional thing! What has that odd-looking Chinaman done to you that you would want to be a man?" she asked, her tone one of pity. "I certainly hope that beast hasn't befouled your innocence."

Andrew felt his anger flare, and at the same time, he felt a jolt that drained him of all his energy when he broke free of Korlue's hold. He hit the floor, and Madame Delphine gasped in response.

"Well," she said, her powder-white, arrogant nose in the air. "At least you know how to handle your rabid dog."

Andrew groaned as he felt Korlue pull him up. He glared at the hateful old woman. "May I kill her?" he growled.

"Not with all these witnesses around," Korlue replied politely, smiling at the few frightened patrons in the store.

Madame Delphine's mouth gaped open in shock. Andrew hated her, and she disliked him. But though it was hard to tell at times, she liked Korlue. Everyone did; it was hard not to. Korlue was smart, beautiful, bubbly, and kind. Andrew adored him and doted on him every day.

"Please, Madame. Is there anything I can help you with? Perhaps a new book?"

She waved him off dismissively. "No, dear. I only wanted to visit and check on you," she started casually. "I was hoping you would have gotten rid of that," she pointed her gnarled, spindly finger at Andrew, "by now. He's no good for you, and you should be with your own kind. Perhaps—"

"Madame! Enough! Andrew is my mate, and I love him very much. I would never get rid of him," Korlue fussed, still holding Andrew.

Korlue had put more of a charge in that little zap than he realized. Andrew knew he would have to feed to recover faster. His kind were weak against lightning, and last time it took him a full day to get his energy back when Korlue shocked him to prevent the immediate murder of a customer.

"If you say so, dear. But I won't give up on you. You're much too sweet and lovely to be bound to that animal. I will break whatever spell it has cast on you. Mark my words," she said as she left the shop.

Korlue breathed a sigh of relief when she left. "Come on, honey. Let's get you to the back room to rest."

"You should have just let me eat her," Andrew grumbled.

Korlue laughed bitterly at that. "I would have, but people would talk, and I'd rather not have you get arrested," he replied, laying him down on the cot they had set up in his office near the back of the store.

"I would be doing this city a favor by getting rid of her," he mentioned.

"Yes, but at what cost? I couldn't bear it if I lost you again."

Andrew sighed as he settled onto the cot. He understood Korlue's concern. It had been nearly four years since he had lost control of his body to Dorjan, a fallen god, and he had died at the hands of Roland Ausher because of Dorjan's thirst for revenge. He did not understand what had happened or why, but when he thought he was permanently dead, he was revived. He assumed a goddess had taken pity on him. Whatever the reason was, he was grateful. Raesh had died that night, but Andrew was alive and back with his love, and they had a life together. Something he never thought would be possible for him.

Andrew was an Andr, and the last of his kind. Once, long ago, he was an assassin, slipping through the shadows of cities and streets. Later, he used his daggers for daring stunts as a circus performer, dazzling crowds with feats that drew from his draconic agility and skills as a martial artist. And now? Now he spent his evenings carefully stacking books and offering acupuncture sessions he learned from his days as a pirate to those brave enough to trust a man with hands as steady as his dangerous past.

Korlue, his lightning elemental dhampir lover and co-owner of Bound to Please, was the firecracker of the shop—figuratively and literally. Where Andrew was steady and deliberate, Korlue was a whirlwind of motion, darting from one task to another, never quite staying still. His energy was infectious, lighting up the shop with his quick wit and the occasional actual lightning bolt when he got overly excited, which happened more often than Andrew liked when they were near their more flammable inventory. Despite the grounding charm Andrew had given him years ago, Korlue's power was sometimes difficult to contain. Korlue's laughter, bright and sharp, would echo through the shop, harmonizing with the distant sounds of jazz drifting down the cobblestone streets.

"What's going on in that pretty head of yours?" Korlue asked, smiling down at him.

"Nothing important," he replied, returning his smile. "Just that I am glad to be with you again." He took hold of Korlue's hand and kissed the back of it.

"That sounds a little important to me," he grinned, sitting on the edge of the cot.

Andrew pulled him down and kissed him, running his hands up and down his back before grabbing his rear.

Korlue pulled back, laughing. "Oh, no, I have work to do out front. You just stay here and rest."

"I would not need to rest if you let me have you," Andrew muttered.

"Yes, I know, but you always take too much after I shock you. And I don't enjoy feeding on blood as you do."

Again, Andrew sighed. "Very well, I will rest."

"I'll come back later to check on you, all right?"

Andrew nodded, and Korlue gave him a light peck on the lips before returning to the storefront. As he watched his lover leave, he smiled to himself. Andrew loved the slight sway of his hips as he walked. With his long white hair, bright blue eyes, and soft pink lips, it was no wonder he was frequently mistaken for a woman. Andrew knew he hated the confusion, but he was slender and pale and absolutely beautiful. It could not be helped.

Slowly, Andrew drifted off to sleep.

All he could do was watch. A storm rolled in, an ominous backdrop behind the Ausher mansion. The air was thick with tension as Roland Ausher faced off against Dorjan Vasary, now happily residing in Raesh's body like a malevolent parasite. Raesh could feel Dorjan's rage and desire to kill his brother where he stood, but he was not yet at full power. Though he had acclimated to Raesh's body, Dorjan was still missing some of his power, and part of Raesh's soul had lingered behind. All that stood between Dorjan and his full godhood was Roland. And he would not let Dorjan anywhere near his family.

Words were exchanged as the wind bellowed around them, then the battle began. Raesh felt as Dorjan summoned his power and watched as his fire, altered by Dorjan's power, clashed with a torrent of water that Roland called forth from the storm clouds and surrounding plant life. Shadows came from nowhere and everywhere, twisting like vines to capture Roland, and Dorjan charged at him with a sword that Raesh could feel pulling on his energy. It had an unnatural weight to it.

Water surrounded Roland in streaming torrents as he defended himself against his brother's relentless attacks. Raesh was helpless, a voyeur in his own body, as a funnel of water sent him and Dorjan reeling back. Even the small fragment of his soul that remained had no control over his body. Yet he could feel every strike, every rush of adrenaline. And the slight increase in weight of the sword.

It was not long before Dorjan landed a near-crippling blow, severely burning Roland and capturing him with shadow tendrils. Before Dorjan could strike with his sword, Roland broke free of the shadow restraints, just barely dodging the killing blow. It was then that Raesh saw a god bleed. Dorjan had cut Roland's arm, and it bled badly. Roland looked scared; Dorjan was going to win.

Dorjan charged at Roland again. He had his brother running scared and keeping his distance. Raesh could tell from the beginning that Roland's heart was not in this fight, but Dorjan did not care. All he wanted was death and vengeance. As the brothers warred, Raesh could feel Dorjan getting weaker, yet he was winning the fight. Then Raesh remembered the blacksmith had cursed the sword with his dying breath. Then, the sword was too heavy to move. And Roland saw his chance.

Pain coursed through his body as his blood seized. Raesh watched in fear as Roland's power over water extended to the blood in his veins.

"It's over, Ozzy," he heard Roland say. "I'm sorry."

Raesh panicked. He wanted to move. To get away. But the fight was over now. He felt a searing pain in his chest, and he choked on his blood. As Roland held him, Raesh's body trembled as Dorjan's words choked in his throat. Soon, his body was swallowed by his altered flames, and then there was only darkness.

Andrew woke up screaming for Korlue. He had fought in his sleep and torn through the cot, and now he lay on the floor. Korlue was quickly at his side, kneeling and making shushing sounds. Andrew had been having that same nightmare for nearly four years. Korlue had always been beside him when he woke to prevent him from burning down the shop and their home. He had tried to remind him that he was Andrew Young now. Sang, Raesh, and David were part of his past and had no place in his new life. Korlue refused to call him anything other than Andrew or Andy. Their shared life was all that mattered now. Andrew needed to let go of what haunted him, but that was easier said than done. He was not the only one having bad dreams. Korlue was fighting his own demons as well.

"I've closed down the store. It's late, let's get you upstairs to bed," Korlue murmured, lifting Andrew up.

They headed out of his office and to the back of the shop where a wrought-iron gate stood, leading to a staircase.

"Are you well enough to go up?" Korlue asked.

Andrew nodded slowly as Korlue turned the knob to open the gate. The stairs led up to their apartment above the store. To the right of the gate was a small study with a floor to ceiling bookcase against the wall near the gate, and a long desk with a chair that sat before it looking out onto the small courtyard through a pair of French doors. They made their way slowly up the stairs behind the gate, stumbling a few times since Andrew was still feeling weak.

Once they made it to their bedroom, Korlue gently eased him into their bed. Andrew sank into the soft, downy bedding as Korlue worked to remove his shoes, and then, his clothes.

When he was completely naked, he tucked him in before disrobing and climbing in beside him. Although Andrew had slept for hours and had remained fairly weak, being in such close contact with his lover's bare flesh still aroused him.

"I suppose I should do something about that," Korlue giggled.

He worked his way under the covers and between Andrew's legs. Andrew felt Korlue's warm hands around his shaft; the light buzz of electricity did not go unnoticed.

"Kory, please," he groaned.

Korlue chuckled. "Sorry."

And without another word, he bent his head to envelope the head of Andrew's cock with his mouth. The wet heat of Korlue's mouth and the erotic sounds he was making caused Andrew to go stiff and swear softly as his hand found its way into Korlue's hair. With his free hand, he pulled back the blanket to watch Korlue at play.

Andrew's eyes lit up at the sight of his cock disappearing into the other man's mouth, stretching out his lips as his head bobbed up and down. He took in the soft sounds of his lover's suckling and muffled moans. Korlue worked him like a greedy, hungry youth with the skill of a much older lover, sucking him with steady, deep and slow pulls of his mouth. His tongue massaged his shaft with expert care.

At this rate, he would not last much longer, and he wanted to feed so he could return his lover's torment. He took hold of Korlue's hair and pulled his swollen lips from his cock, bringing them up to his. He kissed him fervently, thrusting his tongue into his mouth as deeply as he had his prick, lightly nipping his bottom lip when he pulled out.

"I need you," Andrew said, his voice a low rasp.

Understanding what he wanted, Korlue swept his hair aside and bared his throat. "Not too much; I have an early morning."

Andrew ran his tongue across his throat, making Korlue shudder, before sinking his fangs into the taut flesh. He took what he needed and nothing more. The last thing he wanted was to tire his lover out before was ready. He kissed the twin wounds as he rolled Korlue onto his back.

"Feeling better now?" he asked, his bright blue eyes glazed over with lust.

"Much," Andrew replied, his erection stiff and twitching between them as he looked down at his partner.

Andrew took hold of Korlue's narrow hips between his large, calloused hands, and pulled him into the position he needed him in. The head of his cock was still slick from his lover's wonderful mouth, and the clear proof of his arousal. He rubbed it up and down the tight split between Korlue's cheeks. Moving slowly, he teased with quick moments of pressure.

"Andy," he begged, writhing beneath him. "Please hurry."

Andrew smiled at his impatience, but he was just as eager to take him. He slid his full length past the tight, hot ring with relative ease, but still worried that it might have been too fast. Though the sweet sounds Korlue was making removed his worry, and his face had a look of pure ecstasy. Korlue babbled incoherently as Andrew worked in and out of him at a maddeningly slow pace.

"By the gods..." He lost what he was saying on a gasp as Andrew pushed deeper, rubbing the tip of his cock against the sweet spot of his pleasure.

Andrew braced himself against the headboard as he pulled out partially, and then thrust back in, bumping the sensitive spot as he dragged the mushroom tip of his prick against it as he withdrew again and again. Korlue continued to writhe and buck beneath him, strangled sounds of pleasure escaping him.

He pounded him hard, not wasting an inch as each of his strokes brought deep grunts and joyful cries from his lover. He felt his scrotum tighten as he heard Korlue murmuring his name, watching as Korlue's cock pulsed before spilling his seed onto his belly. When Korlue finally went limp, Andrew shut his eyes and pumped his own semen into his partner's quivering ass.

Once he emptied all that he had, he pulled out of him. He leaned over him and laid a gentle kiss on his sweat-soaked brow before getting off of him and going to the ensuite bathroom to retrieve a wet rag. Using the warm cloth, he gently cleaned his lover, who was now unconscious, then returned the soiled cloth to the bathroom hamper. He turned out the lights and crawled back into bed beside his love, smiling when Korlue turned to curl into him. It was not long before he too drifted off to sleep again. This time, his mind was filled with thoughts of their future rather than nightmares of his past.

CHAPTER 3

T heir home was small, and they did not have much, but it was theirs, and they were happy. Nideya was twelve, almost thirteen, and she loved to paint and draw. Her mother, though ill most days, always encouraged her love of art. Elisa was an oracle, and she had passed not only her love of art to her daughter but also her gift of future sight. Nideya could not yet control her gift, and they usually came in the form of dreams or violent visions, like her mother's. She had hoped to gain the level of control her mother had one day.

"Mama, how are you feelin' today?" she asked.

Elisa smiled warmly down at her. "Much better today, Chéri. I see you have been out painting again," she laughed, wiping a smudge of paint off her daughter's face.

Nideya nodded as she giggled under her mother's inspection. "Can I show you?"

"Of course, Chéri! But, later. Go get cleaned up for supper."

The girl pouted at first, but agreed. As she ran off to the bathroom, she saw her mother catch herself on the end of the dining room table, holding the side of her head. She straightened up and smiled when she caught Nideya's worried expression. Reluctantly, Nideya went into the bathroom to wash up.

They ate dinner as if nothing were wrong. Nideya constantly worried about her mother's health. They could not afford medicine or for her to even see a doctor. Still, Elisa smiled and continued to sell her art so they could eat and keep a roof over their heads. She painted beautiful portraits and landscapes. And she made and mixed her own paints using what she found in nature. She even taught Nideya how to make the paints she used. Their life was simple, but Nideya wanted nothing more. So long as she had her mother and her art, she needed nothing else.

After dinner, Nideya brought out the canvas she'd been working on all afternoon. She held it close to her chest as she padded barefoot across the creaky floorboards, her heart fluttering with a mix of pride and nerves.

Elisa sat in her worn armchair by the window, a shawl wrapped around her shoulders, the last of the evening light casting a golden halo around her silver-streaked curls. She looked up and smiled, patting the space beside her.

"Come, let me see what you've made, mon coeur."

Nideya turned the canvas around.

It was a painting of a forest at twilight, but not one from their world. The trees were tall and twisted, their trunks blackened like charcoal, their branches reaching like fingers toward a bruised sky. In the center stood a girl with a crown of thorns, her eyes closed, her hands outstretched, and a faint glow blooming from her chest.

Elisa's smile faltered, just for a moment. She reached out, her fingers brushing the edge of the canvas, then trailing to the girl's glowing chest.

"This light," she murmured. "It's not from the sun."

Nideya nodded. "It's from inside her. I think... I think she's trying to hold something in. Something that wants to get out."

Elisa's eyes softened, though a shadow passed behind them. "You saw this in a dream?"

Nideya hesitated. "I think so. I don't remember it all. Just... the feeling. Like she was scared of what she could do."

Elisa was quiet for a long moment. Then she reached for her paintbrushes, her hands trembling slightly. "May I?"

Nideya's eyes widened. "You want to paint on it?"

"Only a little," Elisa said gently. "Just to help her see."

She dipped her brush into a mixture of ochre and crushed violet petals, then added a faint shimmer around the girl's heart—like a pulse of energy, both beautiful and dangerous. Then, with a few deft strokes, she painted a small figure in the distance: a silhouette watching from the shadows. hand outstretched, not in fear, but in longing.

"There," Elisa said, setting the brush down. "Now she's not alone."

Nideya stared at the addition, her breath catching. "Who is that?"

Elisa leaned back, her eyes distant. "Someone who sees her. Someone who understands."

Nideya looked at her mother, then back at the painting. The girl on the canvas still stood in darkness, but now there was a thread of connection—thin, glowing, like a line of ink drawn between hearts.

"I love it," Nideya whispered.

Elisa smiled, though her eyes shimmered with something unsaid. "So do I."

That night, she dreamed. She wandered through the woods behind their home, following the floating fairy lights as they led her deeper into the forest. The fairy lights whispered to her, but their voices were like tinkling bells, and she could not make out what they were saying. Still, she followed them into the part of the woods her mother had told her to stay away from.

Moving low-hanging branches out of her way, she came upon a dark, shimmery pit in the middle of a small clearing. She shielded her eyes when what looked like a star came barreling down from the sky. It was so bright as it landed in the center of the pit, pulling the fairy lights in with it.

For a moment, the pit was quiet. Then it stirred, swirling and churning almost violently before it exploded. Nideya yelped as what appeared to be ink splashed on her. It did not burn, but it tingled as it seeped into her skin. Her body glowed in the spots where the ink had landed. The pit called to her then, drawing her to it. She knelt on the ground and tentatively touched what remained in the small pit. The ink connected to her fingers, traveling up her arm and into her body.

Frightened, she quickly backed away, but it was too late. The ink had fused with her. Now, her whole body glowed, levitating off the ground. Once her feet were firmly planted, she bolted from the forest and back home.

Nideya woke up breathing hard in a cold sweat. She patted all over her body, checking for any signs of the ink, but saw nothing on her. Breathing a sigh of relief, she pulled back her blanket and got out of bed. After she dressed, she went in search of her mother. She found her out back preparing paints.

"Nideya? You're up early. Is something wrong?" she asked, drying her hands on a rag.

Nideya shook her head. "Just a strange dream."

Her mother gave her a suspicious look, but said nothing more about it.

"May I go into the forest today?"

Elisa furrowed her brow. "Whatever for, Chéri?"

Nideya shrugged her shoulders. "I just have a feelin' somethin' is waitin' for me there."

She gave her daughter a knowing look and a smile. "Of course you may, but be careful," she said, going over to the small wooden table she was drying paints on. "Take this with you." She handed her a medium-sized bottle.

Nideya gave her a confused look as she took the bottle. Before she could ask why she needed it, her mother shushed her.

"You're going to need it, Chéri. Don't worry about the why," she smiled. "Now go."

"All right," Nideya mumbled, still confused.

When she turned to leave, her mother pulled her into a tight embrace and kissed the top of her messy locks. "I love you. I hope you know that."

Nideya scrunched up her face with worry. "I'm just going into the forest, Mama."

Elisa released her, brushing away a tear that ran down her face.

At that, Nideya frowned. "Mama, are you well?"

"Yes, Chéri."

Nideya made a sound as if she did not believe her.

Elisa only smiled. "I promise I'm never going to leave you. Now, off with you."

Nideya hesitated, but her mother smiled and shooed her away. Reluctantly, she made her way into the woods. She followed the path the fairy lights had shown her in her dream, though it looked different during the day. Still, she recognized the trees and kept going. When she moved the low-hanging branches out of the way, knew she was going in the right direction.

After she passed the low-hanging branches, there on the ground was the shimmering ink pit. The closer she got to it, the more it churned and called to her. Just like in her dream, she knelt beside it and reached her hand out. And like before, the ink crawled up her arm and enveloped her body, lifting her from the ground. This time she did not panic; she let the ink absorb itself into her skin.

When she landed back on the ground, the bottle her mother had given her filled with the ink. Amazed, she pulled out the stopper and turned the bottle upside down, but the ink did not come out. She put the stopper back, and then she hurriedly made her way back home.

Nideya burst through the back door, breathless with excitement, clutching the ink bottle like a talisman. "Mama?" she called, her voice bright with hope. Since her mother was no longer out back mixing paints, she went looking in the house. But the silence was thick—unnatural.

She stepped into the house, her boots echoing on the warped floorboards. The dining room was dim, with the curtains half-drawn. A package sat on the table, wrapped in brown paper, with a note pinned to it. She moved toward it, but froze mid-step.

A coldness gripped her spine.

Her mother lay sprawled on the floor, limbs twisted, blood blooming from her eyes and nose like grotesque flowers. Her mouth was slightly open, as if she had tried to speak. Nideya's breath caught. She dropped the ink bottle, not caring if it shattered, and ran to her mother's side.

"Mama?" she whispered, voice cracking. "Mama!"

She dropped to her knees, gathering her mother's limp body into her arms. Her mother's skin was already cold, her hair damp with blood. Nideya rocked her, sobbing, screaming, begging. "Wake up. Please wake up. You promised you'd never leave me."

Her cries echoed through the empty house, unanswered.

Time lost meaning. She did not know when she had passed out, only that when she woke, her mother's body was stiff, her warmth gone forever. Nideya pressed her face into her mother's hair, inhaling the scent of lavender and linseed oil, trying to memorize it before it faded.

No one would come. No one ever did.

They lived too far from the city, tucked into the woods like secrets. And even if she could reach someone, who would help a poor Black woman and her half-breed daughter with cursed blood and visions that only ever brought sorrow? Her mother had painted beauty into a world that refused to see it. Nideya had seen horrors in her dreams, and her mother had tried to paint over them.

Now the house was silent. Her mother was gone.

After a few more moments, Nideya laid her mother's body down and went to the table to get the note. She passed the ink bottle as she did. It had not broken when she dropped it, but she would worry about that later. She picked up the note and choked on a sob as she read it.

My dearest Chéri, if you are reading this, then I am already gone. I'm so sorry to have left you, my love, but you must be brave, and you must be strong. I have packed some supplies that you'll need for your journey. People will be cruel and awful to you because of how you look and because of your gifts, but you must keep going. You will do something great for strangers who will love you as their own one day. I've seen it, so you must believe me. Go to your father in New Orleans. He needs to know that I'm gone and that you are my final gift to him. His name is Henri Moreau, and he is a good man. He has the means to care for you.

Know that I never wished to leave you, but the gods have called for me to rest. You have your whole life ahead of you, and you'll have a grand adventure soon. Don't close your heart, and never give up. I will always be with you; you only need to remember me. I love you, my little one. Now, go be great. And never stop painting.

She crumpled up the note in angry tears. Her mother knew she was going to die, and instead of spending her remaining time together, she sent her out into the forest to follow a dream.

Nideya glared at the ink bottle. Its contents churning inside with its iridescent rainbow shimmer. Did her mother know about the ink pit, too?

Tossing the note aside, she went to unwrap the package. Within it were rolls of parchment paper and the paints her mother had made with some handmade brushes. All neatly packed in a canvas satchel. Nideya broke down in a torrent of tears again. Her mother was gone, and she was on her own.

CHAPTER 4

K orlue stood behind the register, leaning against the counter as he read that day's paper. Several bodies had been found in alleys. Something had drained all the vitality from them, leaving nothing but husks behind all around the city. The majority of them were within the French Quarter or near the docks.

"Whatcha readin' der, Kory?" came a familiar young voice, startling Korlue.

He clutched his chest. "Oh, Lucian!" he gasped. "Don't sneak up on me like that."

"Who's sneakin'?" the boy laughed. "I came right tru da door."

Korlue scowled at the boy, then smiled at the huge grin on his dark face. "What trouble did you bring me today, Luc?"

"No trouble today. But I brought ya some fresh beignets." He set the package he brought on the counter and unwrapped it. "Mama say hi, by da way."

Korlue's eyes went wide at the sight of the large pile of square-shaped lumps of deep-fried dough covered with a generous amount of powdered sugar. He got in close and took a long, deep whiff of the piping hot confections. The sweet, buttery smell had him nearly drooling. He picked one up delicately, being mindful of all the sugar and the heat, and took a bite. The warmth that filled his mouth was heavenly. He quickly stuffed the rest of it in his mouth, then reached for another as he chewed.

"Do not eat too many of those," came Andrew's voice. "You will get sick again."

Korlue waved him off as he started on the second one, moaning with his eyes shut as he took a bite.

"Don't worry, Mista Young. I brought enough for ya, too," Lucian grinned.

"I do not eat such things, and you should not bring them so often," he fussed casually. "He will eat them all and become ill."

"And it will be worth it," Korlue chimed in with his mouth full, popping Lucian's hand when he reached for the pile.

"You know he does not share," Andrew reminded the boy as he walked behind the counter to retrieve the discarded newspaper. He folded it neatly and placed it next to the still-steaming confections.

Lucian picked up the paper, going over the article on the front page. "Did ya'll here 'bout dat body just past Jackson Square?"

Korlue shook his head as he went for another beignet, getting a hard glare from his lover. Which he ignored.

"Dey say she was frozen solid."

"Frozen?" Korlue said, his mouth still full. "In this heat?"

"Yeah, she was shattered into pieces on da ground. Like her blood was frozen," Lucian explained.

"That's so awful!" Korlue covered his mouth before anything came out. "Did they find out who did it?"

Lucian shook his head. "And now we have mo'e bodies pilin' up all around da city."

Korlue perked up at that. "I was just reading about all the husks they've been finding." He scowled as Andrew wrapped up what remained of the sugary pastries and took them away.

"Dey call him da Shade," said Lucian.

"That is a ridiculous name," Andrew sneered. "Why not just call it what it is?"

"Dat's da t'ing," Lucian started. "Dey don't know what it is."

Andrew frowned. "It is quite obviously an incubus," he explained.

"What make you t'ink dat, Mista Young?" Lucian asked.

"They are leaving behind husks drained of vitality, and the victims are both male and female," he said matter-of-factly. "What else could it be?"

"Oh yeah, I forgot 'bout dose t'ings. What 'bout da frozen lady? What did dat?" Lucian wondered.

"Most likely a water elemental with blood control," Andrew answered.

Lucian eyed Andrew with a look of suspicion. "Ya sho know a lot 'bout dese t'ings for a booksella."

Now Korlue was nervous. He and Andrew had not disclosed their past lives to anyone in the area. Most just assumed they were just a bookseller and an acupuncturist. There were of course those who gave Andrew suspicious looks. He had visible scales and many scars. His temper did not help. But they would just assume he was some sort of chimera with demonic origins, and never had the gall to ask him. Their life had been peaceful for the last four years, and

Korlue had made several friends in that time. The last thing he wanted to do was uproot their lives and start over someplace new.

Before he could respond, Andrew put a gentle hand around his waist and said, "There are many books on the subjects of incubi and elementals in this store. Of course I know a lot about such things."

Korlue relaxed against him, lightly covering the hand on his waist with his own.

"Right," Lucian said, with a sly smile on his face. "I suppose dat make sense, seenin' as Kory's an elemental. What kind again?"

Electricity appeared in Korlue's eyes, and the air buzzed around them.

"Korlue," Andrew warned, giving him a light squeeze.

Lucian smiled brightly. "Lightnin'. Got it."

The air calmed, and Korlue touched the obsidian stone in the silver bezel surrounded by small sapphires and metal filigree, hanging from a silver chain around his neck. It was a grounding charm that Andrew had given him years ago. He liked to run his fingers over the runes carved on the back and around the bezel that held the stone.

"Dat's a fancy necklace, Kory. Real pretty."

Korlue smiled warmly at the young boy. "Yes, it keeps me from attracting too much electricity or lightning bolts when I go outside. Andy gave it to me years ago, after he asked me to be his mate." He gave Andrew a chaste peck on the lips.

Lucian leaned on the counter, a dreamy look in his dark brown eyes. "Aww, dat's real sweet. I hope to find my own amour someday," he sighed.

"You are still a child," Andrew mentioned. "Too young to be thinking of such things."

"Don't listen to him, Luc," Korlue chuckled as Andrew removed his arm, grumbling as he did so. "The right girl will come along one day, and you'll make her very happy. Especially if you bring her your mother's beignets."

"And may she be as sweet and lovely as you," Lucian said with a wink.

Andrew narrowed his eyes at the boy before walking off.

"Always a charmer!" Korlue laughed.

"Maybe I'll meet her tonight," Lucian mused.

Korlue gave him a curious look. "What's so special about tonight?"

"Der's a new place openin' up on dis end o' da Tango Belt. You two should come."

In his excitement, Korlue sent a bolt across the counter, nearly hitting Lucian. He covered his mouth in shock. "I'm so sorry!"

"Mon Dieu!" Lucian jumped back before the bolt could hit him.

"Are you all right?" Korlue asked.

"Tout va bien," Lucian assured him. "I promise."

Andrew came rushing back to the front, panic in his jewel-green eyes. "What has happened?

"Not'in to worry 'bout Mista Young," Lucian answered, smiling.

Andrew looked over to Korlue, his worry still apparent.

"It's fine. We're fine," Korlue said with relief.

Andrew frowned. "Please be careful, Korlue."

"I said we were fine; I just got a little excited."

"What caused it this time?" he asked, narrowing his eyes.

"Oh, a new jazz joint openin' tonight. I t'ought ya two might come—"

"No," Andrew interrupted flatly.

"Oh, come on," Korlue pleaded. "We haven't been out dancing in ages."

"No," he repeated. "I dislike jazz, and I dislike dancing."

Korlue grabbed both of his hands and stared into his exasperated emerald eyes. "Please, honey. We never go out. I need to burn off some energy."

Andrew raised a brow. "I can think of better ways to burn off that energy."

Korlue glared at his suggestive tone. "Andrew Young, there is a child present," he fussed.

"I'm fourteen, not a child," Lucian retorted, watching the exchange.

"Please, Andy. I want to go."

"I do not, and there is an incubus on the loose. Remember? A club full of warm bodies is perfect hunting grounds," he tried.

"I'll be safe and I can protect myself now thanks to you."

"I'll be ya escort, Kory, if Mista Young don't mind," Lucian interjected.

Korlue looked at Lucian, then back at Andrew. "See, I won't be alone if you don't come, but I would love it if you did."

Andrew sighed. "No, Kory. I do not want to go."

"Fine," Korlue pouted. "I'll just go without you." He dropped Andrew's hands and turned to Lucian. "Be back here at eight. I'll be ready."

"Now, now, I don't wanna make trouble," he said nervously, slowly backing away with his palms out when Andrew glared at him.

"It's fine. There's no trouble at all," said Korlue.

"Korlue, be reasonable," Andrew pleaded. "It is too dangerous."

Korlue gave him a hurt look. "What happened to the man I fell in love with? The man who didn't fear something as tame as a demon? The man who wanted me as his mate and all that entails?"

He did not mean to cause the hurt in his lover's eyes, but he had grown restless hiding in the store, in their home.

"He died, remember? For you," Andrew replied, his tone flat.

"Andy—"

"Go out and burn off your energy. I will be here hiding from demons," he said as he walked off toward the back of the shop, to the room set up for him to do his acupuncture.

Korlue reached out to him to apologize, but he could not find the words. So, he would go out and try to enjoy a night out. They could use the time apart.

Lucian returned for Korlue at the agreed upon time, and they hopped on a streetcar and headed to the new jazz club Lucian spoke about. Korlue had closed down the store on his own that evening, and had not spoken to Andrew again for the remainder of the day. He dressed in a pair of khaki trousers, a white button-down shirt, and black dress shoes. He had pulled his hair back into a messy French braid that lay over his shoulder.

Though he was young, Lucian was tall and lean, looking slightly older than he was. He was dressed in a pair of loose dark trousers and a plain white shirt. He was handsome with his dark complexion.

Once they arrived at the club, it was nearly nine, and the music was already going. People from all over came out to celebrate the grand opening. Korlue soon lost track of Lucian when he saw a pretty girl walk by. He was on his own in the crowd and found that he was missing Andrew. Feeling forlorn and guilty, he wandered to an empty table near the back, watching everyone else have a good time as the music from the live band filled the air.

Bathed in the amber haze of cigarette smoke and gaslight, the chanteuse leaned into the microphone, her sequined dress catching glints of candlelight as she sang of love—sweet, aching, and forbidden. Her voice curled through the room like perfume, threading longing into the syncopated swing of the jazz quartet behind her. The upright bass throbbed like a heartbeat beneath the piano's flirtatious trills, while the trumpet sobbed in bursts of brass, making even the drunkest hearts sit up and ache.

Korlue sat stiff-backed at the corner table, the velvet of the booth rough against his fingertips, the scent of bourbon and old wood clinging to the air like memory. The argument with Andrew still echoed in his chest—sharp, unfinished. The singer's lyrics—soft betrayals wrapped in velvet—slipped past his defenses and found the raw places. Each note was a blade, each refrain a reminder of what he had said, of the way Andrew's eyes had shuttered when he had pulled away.

A glass clinked nearby. Laughter rose and fell like smoke. But Korlue heard only the ache in the singer's voice, felt only the hollowness where Andrew's warmth had once settled. The rhythm urged his foot to tap, but his chest felt cavernous, echoing with the ache of things left unresolved. It made him miss Andrew that much more, and it irritated him as he fingered his grounding pendant.

"What's with the sour face?" came an unfamiliar voice, deep and rumbling, but slightly gravely.

Korlue looked up to see a strikingly handsome man with near-translucent skin, long black hair hanging around his shoulders like a fine hood, and the most magnetic ice-blue eyes he had ever seen. He had a lean, muscular body barely hidden by the tailored black suit he wore. Korlue could not find the words in that moment as he stared wide-eyed at the beautiful man.

The stranger smiled knowingly, flashing a pair of fangs. "I'm sorry; how rude of me. You're waiting for someone."

Korlue blinked wildly for a moment before regaining his composure. "No," his voice cracked. He cleared his throat and tried again. "No, I'm not."

Again, the stranger smiled. "Good, I would hate to intrude. May I sit?"

Korlue gestured to the empty seat in front of him. "Please."

The stranger moved with fluid grace as he moved to sit down. Korlue assumed from the way he spoke and moved that he had to be an old vampire. He had the fangs, the elegance, and the pale skin. He was also gorgeous.

"Is there something on my face?" he asked, chuckling.

"What?" Korlue asked, bewildered. "No, of course not. I'm sorry, I don't mean to stare."

"It's all right, I'm used to it," he smiled. "Can I get you a drink?" he asked, summoning a waitress.

"Oh, no, I don't drink," Korlue blushed.

The stranger whispered his order to the flushed girl, who was grinning from ear to ear, then he returned his attention to Korlue. "Now, about that sour face?"

Korlue furrowed his brow. "Hm? Oh, it was nothing," he replied, playing with his pendant idly.

"Didn't seem like nothing," he countered. "Someone upset you? Was it the young one you came with?"

"No," Korlue laughed. "He's just a friend. I have—" He sighed and regarded the stranger with a smile. "I have no idea what I'm doing here. I came out to have a good time and dance, but here I am sulking."

The waitress came back with two drinks on her tray and the same flushed look and grin. He took the drinks and slipped her a couple of bills. The girl reluctantly went away after the stranger turned and handed Korlue one of the drinks.

"Oh, no thank you," Korlue said.

"Don't worry, it's just club soda. I thought the bubbles might help improve your mood," he admitted.

Again, Korlue blushed. "Thank you; that was nice of you." He took the drink and took a sip. He smiled as the bubbles tickled his nose.

"There, mood improved," the stranger smiled.

"Thank you again," he said, returning his smile.

The music slowed to a sultry tune, and Korlue found himself tapping his foot and swaying along to the rhythm of the bass.

"May I have this dance?" the stranger asked, standing and holding out his hand.

Surprised, Korlue declined. "I don't want people to think ill of you for dancing with a man."

The stranger leaned in close, and Korlue could smell the sea and a hint of death on him. "I don't give a damn what anyone here thinks," he said.

Korlue felt his skin warm, and he allowed the stranger to pull him onto the dance floor. The stranger held him close, and Korlue felt the taut muscles beneath the fine material as they swayed to the music. When he saw they were being stared at, Korlue turned his head to stare at the stranger's chest.

"Don't let them get to you. Just be in the moment with me," the stranger whispered in his ear.

Korlue could feel the stranger's erection straining against him as they danced. Now he was as flushed as the waitress. It was not his intention to lead the stranger on, but he appreciated the attention all the same. "So, are you from here?" he asked nervously.

"No," the stranger replied simply.

Korlue felt hot all over. "Oh, so do you live here or are you just visiting?" His attempt to make small talk made the stranger chuckle softly. He must have known he was nervous.

"You should relax. Didn't you say you came out to have a good time?"

Korlue nodded, still not making eye contact. "What do you do for work?"

Again, he chuckled. It was such a melodic sound, even with the rasp. "I'm a merchant sailor."

"Really?" Korlue looked up at him then. "What do you sell?"

"Nothing special, really. Just this and that," he replied.

"Oh," Korlue answered. He took the hint that what the stranger sold was not for him to know. "Maybe this was a bad idea," he murmured as he pulled away.

The stranger pulled him closer as he tightened his grip on him. "Not so fast," he growled playfully. "I came here to have a good time, too. You should enjoy yourself; I promise I won't bite."

Korlue blushed at the lust-tinged feral look on the stranger's face. "I'm sorry, but my-"

"Please stay," he interrupted. "For me."

Korlue nodded, and they continued to dance. Korlue eventually loosened up. He would have fun tonight since he did not know when he would go out again.

After another song, the stranger whispered in his ear, "Would you like to see my ship?"

Korlue swallowed hard. What was he doing dancing with another man? It felt wrong, but he was still a little mad at Andrew. Even so, Andrew did not deserve this betrayal. "I'm sorry," he started, pulling away. "I can't do this."

He took off out of the club and ran as fast and as far as he could. He ran until he could no longer run, then crumpled to the ground and cried. After a few moments, he felt a hand on his shoulder.

"Please, I just want to be alone."

"Kory, it's jus' me," said Lucian, coming into view. "Tu vas bien?"

"No, not really," he replied.

Lucian sat down next to him, putting a long arm around his shoulder. "What's wrong?"

"I don't know," he sighed, the sound a rattle in his chest.

Lucian frowned. "Ya miss Mista Young, yeah?"

Korlue wiped the tears from his eyes, sniffling. "Yeah."

"Then let's get ya back home," Lucian smiled, standing and offering his hand.

Korlue took the offered hand and allowed the boy to pull him to his feet. They got on another streetcar and headed back to Bound to Please. He would make things right with Andrew when he got there.

CHAPTER 5

H enri Moreau was a wealthy industrialist who was married with three small children. His wife, a blue-eyed blonde woman, looked as if something rotten had been stuck up her nose permanently. Her name was Eleanor, and she was another stuck-up high-society woman who constantly schemed to get ahead. Nideya could tell that Eleanor did not like her at all, but that had more to do with the condition in which she showed up at their home and the fact that her husband had an illicit affair with a colored servant that resulted in a half-bred child. It did not help that Nideya was Henri's firstborn and therefore had first right to his fortune over Eleanor's children. Something Nideya did not care about in the least little bit. She just wanted a family and a place to belong.

When Nideya arrived that afternoon, they had tried to send her away, but she showed them the wrinkled, tear-stained note her mother wrote. Henri whispered Elisa's name in shock, and Nideya could see the hurt in his eyes at her loss. Eleanor saw it too. They fought over her staying with them for a full week, and Eleanor refused to let her children near the 'unclean bastard' in their house. She was also concerned about what the neighbors would think.

"People will talk!" Eleanor screamed. "You must think of the future of your legitimate children."

Henri sighed in frustration. "Ellie, please. She has nowhere else to go, and she is my daughter."

"What if she's lying?" Eleanor demanded. "She just wants your money. That's what they all want."

"I'm sure that's not true," he countered.

"Then why send her now? I bet the bitch isn't even dead. She's probably hiding somewhere until she gets the money."

A familiar rage filled Nideya as they argued in the hall down from the room Henri had set her up in. She heard a loud slap as skin connected with skin, then Eleanor made a sound as if she had been struck. Briefly, there was silence.

"Ellie, I'm sorry. I didn't mean—"

"Save it, Henri," she hissed.

"Come on, Ellie, please."

Nideya heard their voices rise, even as they walked away.

"I want her out!" Eleanor shouted.

Henri sighed loudly; he sounded tired.

A gentle knock came at her door shortly before it opened.

"May I come in?" he asked.

She looked up at him from the floor where she was drawing. "It's your house."

"Yes, of course it is," he said, clearing his throat. He moved to sit on the bed, adjusting himself until he was comfortable. "What are you drawing?"

"Nothin', it's just a sketch."

He smiled. "May I see?"

"I guess," she sighed, handing him the paper.

He laughed softly. "It's a rather good likeness of Eleanor. How she truly looks."

"It's not very good, though," she muttered.

"I think it's brilliant, actually," he said. He handed the drawing back to her. "You don't care for her, do you?"

"She don't care for me," she countered.

"No, I suppose she doesn't," he said wistfully. "I'm sorry if you heard all of that."

"It's fine," she said, packing up her supplies. "I'll leave in the mornin'."

"No, please stay. I can handle Eleanor, and she'll come around eventually," he tried, stopping her from packing. "She just needs time to get used to the idea."

"But people will talk," she repeated in a scandalized tone, mocking his wife. "I won't stay where I ain't wanted."

"I don't care what people say about us. And you are wanted here, at least by me," he said, urgency in his voice. "Please stay, Nideya. I want to get to know you." He knelt on the floor and took her by the hands.

The moment he touched her, her eyes rolled back, then turned white. It had come so suddenly, her vision, and she scrambled for a piece of paper, a brush, and her bottle of ink. She painted feverishly, each stroke deliberate. Final.

By the time she was done, her eyes had returned to normal, and she felt as if a weight had been lifted, but that was how it always was for her ever since she had come into her powers. When she looked up from her painting, she saw a look of absolute horror on Henri's face, and he had gone pale.

"Y-you have y-your mother's curse," he stammered, backing away.

She suddenly felt sick. He called her visions a curse, just like everyone else in the city did when her mother went to sell her art.

He pointed to the bit of paper she used. "What is that? What does it mean?" he demanded.

What poured out onto the paper was not simply a vision; it was a warning etched in shadow and sorrow. Nideya's brush had moved with a frantic, almost divine urgency, painting not with intention but with compulsion. And when it was done, the ink shimmered with an unnatural light, revealing an image too dreadful for her father to comprehend at first. She did not understand what it meant, but she could feel what it was warning about. A home split in two by a jagged fault line, as though the earth itself had rejected the harmony once hoped for. There was a figure resembling her father, kneeling amidst ash and broken glass, clutching the ruins of a cradle—empty. His wife was depicted with her mouth agape in a scream, eyes wide with grief, surrounded by encroaching shadowy figures bearing no faces. Above them, a dark moon and a flock of black birds wheeling in chaotic patterns.

He got up and pulled her up by her dress collar. "What is that?" he repeated. "Tell me now!"

"I don't know," she lied. She did not owe him anything. "I just paint what the ink and vision tell me." That was the truth. The ink had bonded with her, living in her body like a parasite, whispering horrors to her. Demanding she paint them. The ink strengthened her visions. Perhaps she was cursed.

He released her then, backing out of the room. "I want you out of my house by morning," he said. "And never darken my door again."

She glared at him until he was gone, slamming the door behind him. Once she was sure he was out of the hall, she broke down crying. There was nowhere else for her to go. Her mother had no family that she knew of, and she did not have a cent to her name. But she remembered her mother's note. She had to be strong; she had to be brave, because by morning she would be on her own.

CHAPTER 6

S everal days had passed since Korlue's night out. He had relayed that evening's events to Andrew, including his dance with the handsome stranger. Korlue apologized profusely that night, and to his surprise, Andrew did not get upset. He was not sure whether he was happy about his lover's lack of reaction or disappointed. His feelings changed when Andrew took him. It had been a little while since he had been fucked so thoroughly. It was as if Andrew was reminding him of what he had at home. Perhaps he was upset after all. Korlue was sore the next morning when he opened the store, but he was happy about it.

That afternoon, the heat rose off the streets, and people stayed indoors to keep cool. Korlue stood behind the counter fanning himself with a folded newspaper as he blotted the sweat from his brow with a rag. The faint sounds of jazz could be heard through the streets, and he did his best to enjoy the music, but even the wail of the trumpet sounded as if it was melting.

Andrew had left the shop after helping his last client for the day. He had been extra attentive in the last couple of days, not wanting Korlue to feel like their relationship had soured. He had planned to make dinner that night and was out gathering the supplies he needed. Korlue had never once thought of leaving Andrew, even when he was angry with him, but the dragon was still adamant about showing him how much he was still loved and wanted. Korlue smiled and welcomed the attention.

The bell on the front door sounded, drawing his attention from his thoughts. In stepped a tall figure wearing a dark hooded cloak, his face covered with a mask. New Orleans was full of strange characters, but it was far too hot to wear such things. The stranger stumbled slightly and swayed a bit before he made it to the counter.

"Are you all right?" Korlue asked, moving to come assist them. But a large hand came up to stop him.

"I am fine," came a harsh rasp from beneath the hood. "But I have another matter I require your assistance with."

"Of course, I'll do my best to help."

The man straightened up and cleared his throat. "I'm looking for information on any kind of relic that can heal any wound and remove poisons from the body."

Korlue perked up. "Oh, a water elemental can help with the poison," he offered. "But as for wounds, a physician would be best."

The man sighed tiredly. "I have tried removing the poison, but it remains troublesome. The wound is old and still lingers. It causes me a great deal of pain, and no physician can help."

Korlue furrowed his brow. "Hmm, perhaps my mate can assist you, then. He works wonders with his acupuncture."

"No," he snapped, sounding frightened. "Please, I need something with magic to cure me and make me whole again. I was told that your shop would have what I'm looking for."

"Sure," he said, concern in his tone. He looked at the plain black mask the stranger wore that covered his face. It made Korlue wonder if there was something wrong with his face that warranted hiding. "I have many books with different relics that might help you, but it will take me some time to find them all. Are you sure a doctor can't help you or maybe a powerful witch? I know a couple that might be able to—"

"I thank you for your kindness," he interrupted. "But I have had this condition for a very long time, and no one has been able to help me."

Korlue frowned, knitting his long fingers together. "All right, give me a few days to collect what you need."

He was not sure, but from the look in his eyes, the stranger was smiling. "Thank you so much. I shall return in three days for the books." He took Korlue's hand and brought it to the silver lips of the mask.

Korlue blushed as he stared into ice-blue eyes. It was then that he recognized the man. He was the vampire from four nights ago. The stranger even had the same scent, but the smell of death was slightly stronger. He wondered what had happened between that night and now that had changed. Before he could ask, the stranger turned and left. As he was leaving, Andrew was coming in. They passed each other silently, and Andrew acted as if he had not noticed the other man.

When he saw Korlue staring wide-eyed, he turned to watch the stranger leave, then turned his attention back to Korlue. "Something wrong?" he inquired, his arms full of bags filled with meats and vegetables, and other things.

Korlue shook his head, blinking wildly for a moment. "No, sorry for staring."

Andrew raised a curious brow. "Are you certain? Did that customer say anything to upset you?"

"No, but he was sick, and asking for books on magical relics that could cure him," he explained.

"That would explain the smell of decay in the store," Andrew replied. "Whatever he has, it is killing him."

"You can tell that from his scent?" he asked, bewildered.

Andrew nodded, adjusting the bags in his arms. "His scent was also familiar."

Korlue froze. Did he remember the scent from the stranger because it was on him the other night?

Andrew narrowed his eyes at Korlue. "You are behaving strangely. Are you certain nothing is wrong?"

He saw a look in his mate's eyes. There was an almost dangerous luster as the green irises darkened. As if they dared him to lie.

"I'm just worried about the poor guy," he said. It was the truth; he was worried about him, but he could not bring himself to tell Andrew who he thought the stranger was.

"Very well. I will go prepare dinner," he replied after a moment, then moved to go to the back of the store.

Korlue watched him leave, his heart filled with guilt. He did not understand why he could not tell the man he loved who the other man was, and that he wanted to see him again. Remembering the feel of the stranger's erection against him made Korlue flush as the heat of arousal filled him. He remembered it was long and thick, and he found himself wondering what it would taste like—feel like. The vampire was gorgeous and would no doubt have made an amazing lover. He had offered to show Korlue his ship, and Korlue knew there would have been more had he accepted the tempting offer, but the man was not well—though he looked fine that night. He must have fed well. And Korlue was taken.

He shook his head again and slapped himself for the lurid thoughts of being with another man. He loved Andrew, and was committed to him, but part of him would always wonder what it would have been like to be with the handsome vampire. Korlue sighed. Always the whore.

Dinner that evening was nice. Andrew had prepared a delicious Creole dish. There was a mixture of celery, bell peppers, and onions. Creole seasoning was used with smoky andouille sausage and chicken. There were finely diced tomatoes, all mixed with rice and a nice chicken broth. The added taste of garlic balanced out the flavor of the dish. But Korlue ate very little, his guilt over his thoughts of the vampire stranger eating at him. He hid it well; he thought. Andrew did not seem to notice his melancholy. Andrew talked about his day while he was out. He saw to a few patients before going shopping. He mentioned that one old man that he helped with his needles swore that his acupuncture saved him from a hex that had turned him into a frog for the last four years. Their business was not always bustling, but the stories? Those were never in short supply.

When he asked about his day, Korlue did his best to sound cheerful, telling him about the horror that was Madame Delphine Dubois and her constant nonsense. He had barely got the old lady to leave so he could close up.

"Dinner was wonderful and delicious," he started. "I'm sorry I couldn't eat more. I shouldn't have filled up on the sweets that Luc brought earlier." He smiled brightly at his lover.

Andrew returned his smile. "Perhaps the boy should not have brought so many for you."

Korlue laughed. "He really shouldn't. I'm an absolute fiend when it comes to sugar."

"That you are," he agreed, still smiling.

"I am in desperate need of a shower. Did you need help cleaning up?"

"No," he answered. "Go and clean yourself. I will be there when I am done."

"Thank you!" He got up and gave him a kiss on the cheek before running off to their bedroom.

When he got to their room, he stripped down and went into the bathroom. He started the shower, waited for the water to warm, then stepped in. Letting the water rush over him, his thoughts wandered back to the sexy vampire again. He closed his eyes and imagined him there in the shower with him. His long, lean body pressed firmly against his, the cool touch of his pale skin merging with the heat of the water. Korlue wrapped his hand around his shaft, and stroked it lightly, pretending that it belonged to the vampire. He imagined the stranger's lips on his neck and should while his free hand caressed him. The thought of the stranger's bite sent him over the edge.

Panting, he fumbled with the shower knobs to turn the water off. Leaning against the tile wall briefly, his guilt over his little fantasy enveloped him. He stepped out of the shower and grabbed a towel to dry his hair and one to wrap around his body. He released a long breath, then walked out of the bathroom and back into the bedroom. To his surprise, Andrew was there, leaning against the door frame.

"Oh, I didn't hear you come in."

"You were still in the shower when I came in. I was going to join you, but you came out," he explained. He had a strange luster in his dark green eyes as he eyed the towel. "Remove that."

Taken aback, Korlue looked over to the large windows. The curtains were still open, and anyone high enough could easily see in.

"Korlue."

His mouth was suddenly dry, but he slowly unwrapped the towel, letting it fall to the floor.

Andrew's dark eyes gave him a once-over, as if inspecting him. "Come to me."

Korlue tried to ignore his nerves, wondering if Andrew had heard him in the shower as he walked over to stand in front of him.

"Turn."

Nervously, he turned his back to Andrew, feeling him step up behind him. Andrew did not touch him but leaned forward. Korlue could feel the warmth of his breath near his ear.

"Are you tired?" he asked, his voice low, seductive.

Korlue shook his head, too nervous to speak.

"Would you like me to leave?"

Again, he shook his head, gnawing on his bottom lip.

"I want you on the bed," he ordered. "On your belly."

A shiver ran down his spine as he did what he was told. Korlue turned his head to watch as Andrew moved to close the curtains and turn off the lamps. It was all he could do not to wriggle and squirm, but the anticipation was killing him. He had an idea of what was going to happen, but the wait was torture.

"Stop moving."

He could feel him standing over him, watching him closely.

"Your mind has been elsewhere all night," he said softly. "Even though you did nothing to betray your thoughts, I could tell."

Korlue froze at that. There were old books he had found on Andr, and none of them mentioned mind reading as a trait. "Andy, I can explain—"

"Be silent," he commanded. "You were thinking of the man you met the night you went dancing. I could smell him all over you then." His voice was almost a growl. "Tell me," he purred, running his fingers over the curve of Korlue's hip. "Were you thinking of him when you pleasured yourself in the shower?"

"Andy, please," he begged.

"I said be quiet," he growled. "You can imagine how irritating it was to smell him again in the store."

So, he did notice after all, and now he was angry. Tears welled up in Korlue's eyes, then he felt Andrew's mouth at the small of his back before he ran his tongue up the entire length of his spine. He now had him pinned down with his larger, heavier body, stretching his arms out.

"Do you still desire me?" Andrew asked quietly.

Korlue sobbed silently, too frightened to answer.

"Answer me," he said patiently.

He could feel Andrew's eyes boring into him. When he still did not respond, he pressed his weight into him more.

"Now, Korlue," he demanded, his patience slipping.

"Yes," he croaked out. "Please don't hurt me."

Andrew sighed. "You know I would never harm you."

He sounded almost hurt.

"Do you want me to leave?" Andrew asked after a moment, lifting his weight slightly.

"No," Korlue sniffled.

Korlue felt the light brush of Andrew's fingers on the back of his neck as he moved his hair aside. He then placed a tender kiss on the side of his neck that sent a shiver through Korlue's body.

"May I have you now?"

"Gods yes," he breathed.

Andrew put his hand under him and pulled up his hips a little off the bed. He used his free hand to release himself from the confines of his trousers, then guided the head of his cock between the crack of his ass. He poked at the tender opening, pressing against the tight ring of muscles but did not enter.

Korlue rotated his hips in an attempt to convince him to give him more.

"I have been thinking of how we have been together for so long," Andrew murmured, his breath hot against the back of his neck. "Of how I have become docile, and complacent with our life here." He rocked his hips back and forth. "I have not claimed you as mine in quite some time. And now that I have you completely at my mercy, that will change."

His words were dark, his tone silky, and Korlue quivered with excitement.

"I will mark every inch of you tonight," he said. "You are mine, Korlue. Now and forever."

With one smooth thrust, he pierced his body. He pushed deep, pulling Korlue's hips up as his hands held him in place until he forced his entire length into his tight little ass. He then put one hand under Korlue and slid it up his chest, and Korlue's thighs spread across his.

Kissing his bare shoulder as Korlue wiggled against him, he put his cheek to his. "Touch your cock."

Korlue moaned as he unclenched his fists and wrapped his hands around the source of his arousal.

"Stroke it for me." He flexed inside of him when he did what he was told, and thrust back and forth. "Faster. Yes, just like that. How does it feel?"

Korlue was not sure what he meant. Was he talking about the way his phallus was stroking him all the right ways or the way his own hands were tormenting his body at Andrew's command?

"Yes," he sighed. "It feels so good. I love the way you feel inside me. I love you."

Korlue felt Andrew tense up before bringing his hands down to cover Korlue's over his straining erection. Andrew forced him to stroke himself harder, moving his hands slower.

"No, not yet," he whispered. "Do not come."

"Andrew."

"I said not yet," he growled, working himself harder inside Korlue. "Keep stroking yourself while I fuck you. For every second you thought of him. For every time you wished it was him inside you."

Korlue groaned and gasped as Andrew continued his sweet torture, all while Korlue jerked himself.

"Do you wish he were here fucking you instead?"

When Korlue twisted and ground himself down on him, Andrew quickly pulled out of him and put one of his thick fingers into him instead, grabbing the back of Korlue's neck.

"No!" he cried out. "Please, I only want you." He needed him back inside of him, but he continued to fuck him with his finger.

"Now, Qīn'ài de. Now you may come," he said, his voice dark. "Come for me."

It was as if he had been freed from invisible ropes, and Korlue came howling as he felt Andrew's cock twitching and jerking against his bottom. They both spilled their seed, Andrew rubbing his into the sensitive ruck of Korlue's rear with long, maddening strokes of his shaft.

Gently, he laid Korlue down on the bed, facing up, and laid on top of him. He was still hard, Korlue noticed. His dragon had amazing stamina.

Andrew covered his mouth with his, rubbing his still engorged member again Korlue's. His lips trailed along his jaw, then to his throat before stopping in the space where his neck and shoulder met. Korlue cried out, clawing at Andrew's back when he bit down on him. He did not draw blood, but Korlue knew there would be a mark left behind. Andrew continued his descent, his tongue laving his nipple when he got to his chest. Again, Korlue cried out when he bit down on him before moving onto his side where he bit into him again.

By the time he was done, Andrew had left several bite marks all over Korlue's body, all while caressing and fondling him. Korlue came a second time when Andrew bit him on the inside of his thigh, leaving behind little rumbles of ecstasy, like pleasure aftershocks. He shook while Andrew's touch kept them radiating throughout his body. Yet somehow he was not done with him. He made an absolute mess of Korlue, and he was not done. He was punishing him for the infidelity of his thoughts, and Korlue welcomed it.

"Please, mercy," Korlue begged, grinning.

Andrew smiled devilishly at him. "No." He lifted Korlue's legs onto his shoulders, then eased back into him, past the stubborn ring of muscles, inch by glorious inch.

He continued to ride Korlue hard until he filled his rear full of his semen, and he finally softened. At last, he collapsed in exhaustion at his mate's side. Korlue was thoroughly satisfied with his claiming as he fell into unconsciousness next to his love. He would think of a less tiring way to thank him when they recovered.

CHAPTER 7

The air hung thick and humid over New Orleans, heavy with the scent of magnolia, rum, and river rot. The city pulsed with contradictions—decadence and decay, jazz and judgement, freedom and fear. The French Quarter was alive with music and mischief, but beneath its charm lay a darker rhythm.

Nideya emerged from the alley behind a curio shop, her satchel bulging with stolen paints and brushes. She had watched the old shopkeeper nod off in the heat, her head drooping like a wilting lily. It was too easy. But guilt did not slow her steps.

She weaved through the crowd, past the vendors hawking pralines and voodoo dolls, past a preacher shouting about salvation. Her boots echoed on the cobblestones as she found a spot beneath a wrought-iron balcony on Royal Street that was draped in Spanish moss. It was the kind of place where fortunes were whispered and secrets were traded for a nickel.

The gas lamps flickered as if they were unsure whether to stay alive, casting amber halos in the humid dusk. Jazz spilled from a nearby speakeasy, the trumpet's wail curling through the alleyways like smoke. She laid out her stolen tools with care—rolls of paper, oil paint, and a handful of charcoal sticks she wanted to try. Her sign, hastily scrawled on the back of a discarded flyer for a jazz revue, read: I'll paint your future. Pay what you can.

At first, it was a novelty. The city thrived on spectacle. A Creole woman in a peacock-feathered hat approached, her perfume thick as molasses. She offered a silver dime and sat; her gloved hands folded in her lap.

Nideya studied her face, then began to paint.

The brush moved as if it knew more than she did. Colors swirled; shapes emerged. When she was done, the canvas showed a grand ballroom submerged in water, chandeliers shattered, dancers floating like ghosts.

The woman gasped. "That's the St. Charles Hotel," she whispered. "I'm to be married there next month..."

She left without her painting.

More came. A jazz drummer with calloused hands. A bootlegger with a crooked grin. A child clutching a ragged doll. Nideya painted them all, the ink her blood commanded her to, and each canvas told a tale of ruin. A snare drum split in two beside a grave marked with a trumpet. A warehouse engulfed in flames, crates of liquor exploding like fireworks. And a doll abandoned in a flooded street, its eyes staring at the sky.

She tried to paint joy—a parade, a wedding, a sunrise—but the brush resisted. It dragged her into the shadows. Her fingers trembled. Her heart pounded. She did not know where the visions came from, only that they felt true.

The crowd began to shift; curiosity curdled into fear.

Someone muttered, "She's touched by the Loa... but not the good kind."

"She's cursed," said another.

The priest she passed before crossed himself and spat near her easel. A woman threw salt. A man kicked over her jar of coins. The streetcar conductor stared at his portrait—his own face pale, eyes wide, a streetcar derailed behind him—and dropped it as if it burned.

The music from the speakeasy down the block played on, but it sounded distant now, like a memory. The trumpet's wail was mournful. The laughter had thinned. Nideya sat alone, surrounded by paintings no one wanted. Her fingers were stained with oil and ink. Her eyes burned. She stared at her final painting: a girl in a tattered dress, standing beneath a flickering gas lamp, her shadow stretching into the Mississippi.

She wondered if it was her.

A voice broke the silence.

"You see what others won't," said a man in a wide-brimmed hat, his accent thick with bayou. "That's a gift, child. Even if it hurts."

She looked up. His eyes were milky, blind—but he saw her.

"Come with me," he said. "There's a place for your kind. Not here. Not among the tourists and drunks. But deeper. Where the river runs slow and the spirits speak plain."

Nideya hesitated. The city hummed around her, indifferent. Her canvases whispered.

She gathered her paints. And followed him into the dark.

The blind man led Nideya through the Quarter's back alleys, past shuttered jazz clubs and crumbling tenements, until cobblestones gave way to dirt roads and the city's pulse faded behind them. The air grew cooler, damp with moss and mystery. Spanish moss draped from cypress trees like mourning veils. Fireflies blinked in the dusk like scattered stars.

They boarded a flat-bottomed pirogue at the edge of the bayou. The man rowed in silence, his blind eyes fixed ahead. The water was still, black as ink, reflecting nothing. Nideya clutched her satchel, her fingers brushing the bristles of her brushes like talismans.

"You feel it?" he asked, his voice low.

She nodded, forgetting he was blind, but too frightened to speak. The bayou hummed—not with sound, but with presence. It was like stepping into a cathedral built of fog and bark.

They arrived at a clearing where the trees parted like curtains. A ramshackle cabin leaned against the swamp, its porch sagging, its windows glowing faintly with candlelight. A circle of stones surrounded it, each etched with symbols that seemed to shift when she looked away.

Inside, the air was thick with incense and old stories. Shelves overflowed with bones, feathers, and jars of herbs. A woman sat at a table, her skin the color of river clay, her hair braided with beads and bones. She did not look up.

"She's the one," the man said.

The woman nodded. "I know." She finally looked at Nideya. "Sit, child," she said, gesturing toward a wooden stool.

Nideya hesitantly took the offered seat.

"My name is Celestine Marais. That," she pointed to the blind man, "is Émile Thibodeaux."

She stared nervously at the woman, still clutching her satchel. She did not know what they wanted from her.

The woman smiled warmly. "Your name, child? What is it?"

"Nideya," she answered softly, trying to hide behind her bag.

"Don't be shy, Cher. You were brave enough to come with Émile; know that no harm will come to you here."

Nideya nodded, hearing Émile chuckle behind her.

"She's good at nodding," he said.

Nideya flushed, tucking herself into a ball on the stool.

Celestine and Émile both laughed.

"Welcome to our home, Nideya." She smiled again. "Will you paint for me?"

She shook her head vigorously. "No one likes my paintin's. They keep sayin' I'm cursed."

Celestine made a tsking sound. "You're not cursed, child. And that ink you carry in your blood chose you," she said. "It was made from fairy bones and a fallen star. It was made for you because your mother wished it so."

Nideya's eyes went wide, and she stopped hiding. "You knew my mama?"

Celestine shook her head. "No, little one. I've seen it, just as she had before she died."

"Oh," she said, her voice sullen and her head down.

"Don't be sad, Nideya. Your mother isn't gone; she's always with you," spoke Émile, resting a hand on her shoulder.

"Now, will you paint for me?" Celestine asked again.

"All right, but you won't like it," she mumbled.

Nideya pulled out her supplies.

"Not with the paints, Cher. With the ink. Let me see the power you wield," Celestine insisted.

Nideya pulled out the bottle of ink, the contents churning like it had before, the colors changing at random. Nideya was told to paint—not people, but the bayou itself. She dipped her brush into the ink bottle, and the canvas drank it greedily. She painted trees, the fog, the water—and then, without meaning to, she painted eyes. Dozens of them. Watching. Waiting.

Celestine smile. "You're not just seeing the future. You're seeing truths. Things buried. Things forgotten."

"I don't understand. It's just a bunch of eyes lookin' at the bayou," Nideya said.

"It's more than that," said Émile. "You just can't see it yet."

That was funny coming from a blind man.

"Your powers are still growing, girl," Celestine chimed in. "And as they grow, so will your understanding of them."

"I only paint bad stuff, though."

"No, what you paint isn't bad; it's just the truth. People simply interpret it how they want," she said. "And that's on them."

"We brought you here for a reason. Let us help you learn to better understand your gift and help you grow with it," said Émile.

Nideya agreed to stay and learn.

Each night, she painted. Each morning, the paintings changed. A tree she painted now bore a noose. A cabin window showed a face that had not been there before. One canvas bled.

She learned the bayou was alive—not metaphorically, but literally. It remembered. It spoke. And it had chosen her.

One night, Celestine gave her a final task.

"Paint the thing you fear most," she said.

Nideya hesitated. Her hands shook. She painted herself—alone, surrounded by fire, her canvases burning, her gift silenced.

The painting started to smoke.

Celestine threw salt at it, and Émile chanted. The cabin groaned.

Then there was silence.

The painting was blank.

"You faced it," Celestine cheered. "Now you can choose."

Her choices were either to return to the city, her gift sharpened, her visions clearer—but she would never be welcomed. Or she could stay in the bayou, become its keeper, its interpreter, its voice.

She looked at her hands. At her brushes. At the swamp that had become her sanctuary. And she chose. From that day on, those who wandered too deep into the marsh sometimes found a painting nailed to a tree—of themselves, in a moment not yet lived. Some laughed. Some cried. Some ran. But all remembered.

CHAPTER 8

T he sound of jazz and the scent of coffee, along with the overpowering smell of sugar, assaulted his senses as he left Bound to Please. Humidity clung to him through his clothes. It was too hot to be wearing a hooded cloak and mask, but he did not want the dhampir to recognize him, though it all may have been for nothing. He thought he saw recognition in his eyes at the sight of his. Under normal circumstances, he would not have hidden who he was, but he could not risk being discovered. Not until he was healed and back at full strength.

"Are you feelin' all right, Captain?" asked the small man that appeared from the shadows behind him.

"No, Walter. I am not," he grumbled as he stumbled briefly, walking away.

Walter was immediately at his side then. "Yer lookin' a bit paler than usual, sir. You need to feed."

"I know that," he growled. "This venom in my body is powerful still. I need to find a way to rid myself of the rest of it." He continued to walk, heading towards the Quarter.

"But elemental and dark magic couldn't get it gone. What will you do now?" Walter wondered as he kept pace.

He thought as he walked. He was weak now and needed to feed more often than he used to. Before, he could keep his meals alive for days, but he was dying. There was a powerful venom in his body, and he could not rid himself of it fully. He had experienced the venom before, and was able to remove it with relative ease, but this time, it was different. There was more of it, and it was different from the other. Stronger. He was fortunate that he got any of it out. Keeping himself well fed had kept him alive all this time, but it only slowed the effects of the poison.

"Beggin' yer pardon, Captain, but maybe yer under a blood curse," Walter suggested.

He scoffed. "Considering the man I am and the life I've led, that is entirely possible."

"Maybe killing the one that cursed you will fix you."

He sighed. "I've thought of that, Walter, but I'm in no condition to fight that monster again. I need to find another way."

"All right, then what do we do for now?" Walter asked, stopping him when he swayed. "You need to feed."

He looked down at his first mate and saw the worry in his golden eyes. With his jewel-like eyes and blood-red hair, Walter stuck out like a sore thumb. The Vanita was loyal to a fault and had no fear of him as the rest of the crew had. "I can't hunt during the day, Walter. There's too many people; someone will see. And I'm in no condition to make it back to the ship. I need to rest and conserve what energy I have to hunt tonight."

"Very well, sir. I'll find you lodgings for the afternoon." With a curt nod, Walter disappeared into the shadows.

Once Walter was gone, he spotted a small, furry-looking shadow creature lurking nearby. Watching him. Walter must have left it behind to keep an eye on him while he looked for lodgings. He found a bench and sat down to wait for his first mate to return.

As the afternoon sun beat down on him, he felt weaker. He needed to hunt. And soon. He found he liked New Orleans. It was so easy to find prey. He thought of the waifish dhampir from the bookstore. He had almost had him that night. The night they danced. He had fed well before he went after him. The waif was weak and ignored his blood as a vampire. It was too easy to charm him.

His spies had told him that the dhampir was bored and in need of better entertainment. He could have easily had him that night, but something came over his prey and he ran from him. It was likely guilt; the dhampir was taken, after all. And his spies had informed him that the dhampir's lover had taken him many times since that evening. Still, he would have the dhampir for his own soon enough. Until then, he had to survive and get stronger.

So he would wait, and he would hunt.

As the sun set and evening fell, he prepared himself. Free of his cloak and mask, he stepped out of the seedy, run-down hotel Walter had found for him before going back to the ship. He was able to siphon a small amount of sexual energy from the patrons in the hotel. It was not enough to sate him, but it gave him enough strength back to hunt for the evening.

His hair hung long, draped over his shoulders. He wore black trousers and a matching black button-down shirt. He had undone several of the buttons to reveal the pale skin of his chest. His chest was once well-toned, but the venom in his veins had thinned him out when he did not feed well enough.

Yet he strode around the Quarter with the confidence of an apex predator with nothing to fear. Men stepped aside and women blushed, fanning themselves as he passed. Vagrants scurried away, and the stray animals kept their distance.

The speakeasy he walked into had no name and was tucked behind a butcher shop, its entrance hidden beneath a rusted meat hook and a velvet curtain that smelled faintly of absinthe and blood. Inside, the air was thick with smoke and sin. Jazz curled through the room like fine perfume, mingling with the scent of sweat, bourbon, and something older—something metallic and sweet. He was not the only hunter there that night.

The walls were lined with velvet and shadows. Candles flickered in old gin bottles. A woman laughed too loudly. A man wept into his drink. He walked over to where the band had set up at the far end of the room, beneath a spotlight that seemed to glow from nowhere. They all stared at him as he sat behind the piano.

It was old, the piano, its ivory yellowed, but its wood was polished to a mirror shine. His fingers hovered above the keys—long, pale, elegant. Then, with a breathless hush, he began to play. The first notes were soft, like silk brushing bare skin. A slow, bluesy melody made its way through the room, winding around ankles and wrists, slipping into ears like secrets. Conversations faltered. Cigarettes burned down to ash. The bartender froze mid-pour. Then the band joined in.

His eyes scanned the crowd, looking for his next meal. And then he saw her.

She sat alone at a corner table, half-hidden in shadow. Young, maybe twenty. Delicate, with eyes like storm clouds and a dress the color of dusk. She had not touched her drink.

Her gaze was fixed on him—not with lust, but with something deeper. Hunger. Maybe recognition.

He smiled. It was slow and deliberate, like the curl of smoke from a match. Not warm. Not cruel. Just inevitable.

He kept playing.

The music grew darker, richer. Notes fell like rain, then rose like steam on hot cobblestones. The crowd swayed, entranced. A man laughed, then wept. A woman clutched her chest, whispering a name no one knew. Time bent. Reality thinned.

And still, he played.

His fingers danced faster, coaxing desire and despair from the keys. The room shimmered. The candles flared. The shadows grew teeth.

And still, she watched him.

When the final chord rang out, it was like a bell tolling for the dead. The room sat in stunned silence, eyes glassy, mouths parted. No one moved.

He stood.

He walked toward her, his steps soundless on the floor. She did not flinch. Did not speak. Just watched him with wide, waiting eyes.

He offered his hand. She took it.

They vanished through the velvet curtain into the night.

Their lips and tongues were tangled together. The heat of her desire was radiating off of her in waves, and he felt the earth rumble in response. The warmth urged him on as they stumbled out of the speakeasy and into the back alley. He needed to be inside her. He needed to feed.

"So, shall we take this back to my place or yours?" she said after catching her breath, her hands rubbing lightly against the bare skin of his chest.

He grinned. "I don't think I can wait that long."

Before she could protest, he reclaimed her mouth, using his body to force her back against the wall. He reached under her dress and ripped her panties away. He smiled into her lips when she gasped as his nimble fingers stroked the source of her desire. She was beyond soaked.

Still, she had the strength to push him away. "I'm not comfortable doing it out here. Let's go somewhere more private."

"No," he growled low.

He pressed his body against hers again, pinning her hands between her and the wall. When he went to undo his trousers, he felt something hard hit him in the back of the head. He looked back and saw no one. Then he looked back at her; there was fury in her eyes. The earth rumbled again.

Again, he grinned as he stumbled back. He touched his head and drew blood. "Earth elemental?" He got his answer when a small, sharp stone cut across his cheek. More blood came. "You're not going to make this easy, are you?"

"You won't have my blood tonight, vampire," she hissed, then bolted.

He caught her before she could get more than a few steps away. The blood of others was nothing for him to manipulate.

He took both her wrists and pinned them to the wall. He bared his fangs as he spoke. "I'll tell you a secret," he started, then leaned in close. "I'm not a vampire," he whispered, then ran his tongue across her throat.

A malevolent smile spread across his face when he saw the realization in her eyes when she could not move. He freed himself from the restrictive material of his trousers, then he hiked up her dress and took hold of her legs. He spread them wide as he slid into her, feeling her tense up at the feel of his girth.

"Relax, it'll all be over soon enough," he murmured against the skin of her throat.

A tear streaked down her face as she whispered, "You're the Shade, aren't you?"

He chuckled lightly at the ridiculous name. "Is that what they're calling me?"

He covered her mouth when she started to scream for help. She should have been enthralled by now, he thought. He was weaker than he realized.

His strokes were long and hard as he moved in and out of her. He needed her to want this. To not fight him. So, he removed his hand from her mouth and kissed her. Then, after a few moments, she kissed him back. He released as much of his pheromones as he could muster until she was moaning.

He relinquished his hold on her blood, and she wrapped her arms around his neck. His hands were back to holding her thighs, angling her so he could thrust deeper. His lips remained on hers to ensure she did not scream.

With his focus back on his own need, he felt her walls tighten around him. She was coming, and soon he would have his meal. The earth shook as she climaxed, and he soon followed. His mouth hovered over hers, and the ethereal light of her life force flowed willingly into him.

Once he was done, he dislodged himself from her mummified husk, dropping it to the cold ground. Filled with the power of her vitality, he felt better. Not whole, but better. He stared down at the elemental's remains. The dress she wore looked obscene wrapped around her body now. Her skin had dried and shrunk tightly to her bones.

And even in death, she smiled.

He watched as vines struck through the cobblestone like ghastly tendrils and wrapped around the husk, covering it as they dragged it back into the soil.

He smiled as he walked off. At least there would be no evidence of his kill this time.

CHAPTER 9

The day after his night of claiming, Korlue was once again sore with bite mark bruises all over, but he was happy and satisfied. However, he knew the stranger would return in a few days. He did not want to upset his mate again, but Andrew had said that the stranger was dying, and Korlue still wanted to help him however he could.

Before he could go around the store to look for what he needed, Madame Delphine came bursting through the door. Her thin face flushed as she huffed and puffed. He was grateful Andrew was out visiting a patient. The woman looked as if something had worked her up. After the night they had, he was in no real mood to deal with her. She had a way of putting a damper on his good moods.

"Madame, is everything all right?" he asked, trying to sound concerned.

She quickly met Korlue halfway and took hold of his hands. "Korlue, dear! I have had a vision," she exclaimed, as if it was a rare occurrence. "My goodness, what happened to you?"

When she reached for his shirt collar, he swatted her hand away and took a step back.

She furrowed her brow, holding her hands to her chest. "Kory, honey, what happened? Is that a bite mark? Did that beast hurt you?"

Korlue gave her a sympathetic look. "No, Madame. I'm fine; it's just a love bite," he assured her.

She made a sound as if she did not believe him, then she narrowed her eyes at him before reaching over to touch him again. "You are too thin, sugar," she said as he politely grabbed her hands to stop her from feeling him up. "I need to bring you some better food, dear. To fatten you up a bit. You can't have children as skinny as you are."

"For the hundredth time, Madame, I'm a man and can't bear children."

"Oh, don't be silly! I've seen it in your future. You'll have a daughter, but you'll have to find the right man to be your husband," she insisted.

"Madame, please. You couldn't have possibly seen that. And besides, Andrew doesn't want children. He's not overly fond of them."

"Precisely why you need a good husband."

Korlue sighed in exasperation. "I have a great husband, Madame. Better than I deserve."

"And you're going to need a bigger bosom if you want to catch a decent man and be able to feed his babies properly."

The woman was insane. He was sure of it. Before he could protest her delusions further, the bell on the door rang, and in came Lucian with another package of what was likely more delicious beignets.

"Hey, Kory!" he sang, stopping when he saw Madame Delphine. "Oh, you gotta guest."

She curled up her lip at the sight of the boy, then she turned back to Korlue. "Kory, honey, you should do better about keeping the filth out of your store."

Lucian grinned and stepped behind her. "I agree," he said in her ear. "Maybe you should leave."

Madame Delphine shrieked, clutching her pearls as she backed away. Korlue tried to hide his amusement but failed spectacularly.

"It's all right, he's friendly," said Korlue, stifling a laugh.

"Good heavens, Kory, you're surrounded by animals," she gasped.

Still grinning, Lucian stepped into her space again. "Boo."

Again, she shrieked, and hurried out the door mumbling slurs as she left.

"Good riddance," laughed Lucian.

"Luc, that wasn't nice," Korlue said, still giggling.

"She's not nice," he countered. "What she want today?"

Korlue took the batch of pastries from him, taking a deep whiff of them. He always loved Lucian's mother's beignets. "Oh, just to tell me I was going to have a daughter soon, and that she was going to fatten me up to find a good husband."

"Good t'in' Mista Young weren't here for dat."

"I know, and Ms. Eve's got things covered with fattening me up with her beignets," he said, digging into the package and retrieving one of the sweet treats. "Mm, so good!"

"Where be Mista Young?" Lucian asked, smiling at the pretty girl that walked up to the counter with a handful of books.

Korlue shook his head, smiling at the boy. "He's visiting a patient he helped a few days ago." He rang the girl up and wished her well, then he went to put the beignets behind the counter.

"Need help wit' anyt'in'?" He asked, following Korlue.

Korlue paused for a moment to think. "Actually, yes. I could use some help finding some books for a customer."

"What kind o' books?"

"Ones that talk about relics that can heal any wound," he explained.

Lucian's brow furrowed. "What he need 'em fo'?"

Korlue sighed, frowning. "Andrew thinks he's dying, and the man said he had an old wound from being poisoned that won't heal." He continued, "He said nothing has helped him so far."

"And he t'inks somet'in' in a book will?" he asked. "You gotta lot o' books, Kory."

"I know," he groaned. "That's why I need help."

"All right, don't twist my arm or not'in'," Lucian laughed.

Korlue directed him to where books on the subject were located in one part of the store while he searched another near the back.

It took them two days of searching and collecting before they had a sizable stack of books on various items that could help the dying vampire. Lucian had found a book about an artifact called the Verdant Sigil. According to the book, the Verdant Sigil was grown from the heartwood of the world tree and etched with ancient druidic glyphs. It was a leaf-shaped talisman that changed color with the seasons. When pressed to a wound, it summoned vines and moss to knit flesh and bone, but it could not heal wounds caused by unnatural forces such as void magic or necromancy.

Korlue found a book that seemed more to a vampire's liking. The book was about the Bloodmirror Pendant. It had been crafted by a forgotten blood mage who was looking to reverse death itself. The pendant was a crimson gem encased in obsidian, and it reflected the wearer's heartbeat. As he continued to read, he discovered the pendant transferred the wound from one person to another—a literal act of sacrifice. The pendant also chose who would bear the pain, and could not be bargained with.

The last book Lucian found was an old tome about an artifact called the Tideheart Chalice. It was an ancient vessel forged from deep-sea obsidian and inlaid with veins of bioluminescent coral. This chalice was said to hold the restorative essence of the primordial ocean—an undiluted force of renewal and transformation.

It was forged in a place called the Midnight Abyss long ago, a place in the deepest trenches of the ocean where time fractured and the tides whispered secrets in forgotten tongues. The chalice was created by the Oceanborn, a race of celestial water elementals who once governed the balance between the mortal sea and the ever-changing divine currents. It was meant to heal warriors who had given too much in battle, restoring those who had sacrificed their essence for the sanctity of their realm.

As Korlue continued to read, entranced by the story thus far, the text mentioned that the magic of the chalice was never meant to be wielded lightly. The Oceanborn queen, Seraphis the Tidemother, placed an oath upon it—that renewal must always come at a cost. The chalice did not grant restoration freely. It required a sacrifice—something deeply tied to the bearer's essence. A memory of profound significance, a piece of their strength, or a bond they hold dear must be relinquished to the tides. Only then did the artifact bestow its gift, ensuring that transformation never came without consequence.

He continued to read the old book, but slowly realized that it was most likely just a fairy tale. There was no way something like that existed. The Oceanborn emerged from a forbidden union between Seraphis and an exiled demon named Varion the Fallen, a prince cast from the infernal planes. Varion was meant to drown beneath the crushing depths, banished from his realm after betraying his kind. But Seraphis, a being forged from the first floodwaters, felt something strange in the swirling darkness of his presence—a pull that should not have existed between the celestial tides and the abyssal flame. Against the laws of creation, she fell in love and merged her essence with his, and from their union, the Oceanborn were conceived—beings of both fluidity and hunger, ethereal grace and unbreakable will.

Korlue snapped the book shut and sighed. He stretched and yawned, then stared at the book in his hand. Believing in such things was not who he was, though he loved a good fairy tale romance. Still, the book would be of no help to the stranger. It seemed to be more attuned to water elementals and demons, which he knew were real. But finding the Tidevault—a hidden sanctuary submerged deep beneath the world's last living coral labyrinth—was an impossible mission. If it was even real.

The book was filled with stories of those who used and surrounded the chalice. None of those people sounded real at all. Despite all that, something told him to keep the book in the stack he and Lucian had collected. He was too tired to put it back anyway.

He did not know when he fell asleep, but he woke up with a start, Andrew lying beside him, fast asleep. His jerking awake woke his lover.

"I didn't mean to wake you," he whispered. "Go back to sleep. I need to go close the store." He got up to pull on his trousers.

Andrew eyed him tiredly. "I have already done that. You were asleep at the counter when I came back. I brought you upstairs while you still slept," he grumbled, then yawned.

"Oh," he said, then removed his trousers and climbed back into bed. "Thank you." He gave his scowling mate a chaste kiss on the lips.

"What caused you to fall asleep in the first place?" he inquired.

Korlue yawned, curling up to Andrew, who happily embraced him, pulling Korlue close. "I was looking for books about artifacts that could heal any wound for that masked customer."

Andrew frowned at that. "Why?"

"Because he asked, he's still a customer," he replied, wriggling against him as he snuggled closer. "And he's dying. I didn't think it would hurt."

Andrew grunted and grumbled, making Korlue chuckle softly.

"I promise it means nothing. I only want to help him."

"Fine," Andrew muttered. "Go back to sleep now."

"Wǎn' ān, wǒ de àirén," he smiled into his lips.

Again, his lover grumbled, closing his eyes as he murmured goodnight in Mandarin as well. Korlue let out a contented sigh, then drifted back off to sleep.

CHAPTER 10

I t had been a month since Nideya had come to the bayou. Celestine and Émile had welcomed her when no one else had. They showed her she had nothing to fear of her gift. She had learned that Celestine was a root worker, a spiritualist descended from a long line of Creole mystics. She was born during a thunderstorm and raised by her grandmother, who taught her to read bones and brew potions that could heal or hex. She was fierce, maternal, and enigmatic. Celestine was the kind of woman who could make you feel safe and terrified in the same breath. Her laugh was rare, but when it came, it was like wind through the cypress.

Émile was a different story. He was once a trapper and folk healer who lost his sight in a fire that spared his cabin but took his family. When he took Nideya back to the city to help get supplies, she overheard the locals say he saw more now than he ever did with his eyes. He was known in the swamp as a 'listener'—someone who heard the spirits when they whispered through the reeds. Émile was stoic, poetic, and deeply intuitive. He rarely spoke unless it mattered. When he did, it was with the weight of someone who had lived many lives.

Nideya was learning so much from the pair, but even still, she was feeling restless.

"What's the matter, child?" asked Celestine.

Nideya looked at the woman over the plate of sausage, eggs, and grits, and grumbled tiredly as she poked at her food.

Celestine smiled wryly. "You had the dream again, didn't you?"

Nideya nodded, finally taking a bite. She had been dreaming of people she did not know in a shop she had never been to. Each dream told her something more about them and the world they lived in. There were two men, lovers, and they ran a bookstore together. The store was huge and filled with many kinds of books on shelves that reached the ceiling. It looked like a magical place, but the owners had dangerous pasts.

From what she could tell, one was a fancy man, and the other was a killer. Her dreams had shown her that they had somehow gotten tangled in a feud between two powerful beings, and the killer sacrificed his life to save the fancy man. A pure light revived the killer, and he found the fancy man. And though that fight was long done and that chapter in their life was closed, danger still surrounded them. Hunted them. It all seemed like a bizarre fairytale.

"Why not paint your dreams? Get them out of your head," Celestine suggested, interrupting her thoughts. "It might help you understand them better."

"They're just weird dreams. They don't mean nothin'," she mumbled, poking lazily at her food again.

"How would you know?" Celestine argued, leaning on the table.

Nideya sighed. "Fine, if you think it'll help."

That afternoon, after a much-needed nap, Nideya set up her easel and one of the stretched canvases Émile had picked up for her. Then, she painted. The dreams had been vivid, and she painted them all, the ink in her blood and the bottle stirring almost violently as she moved from canvas to canvas.

By the time she was done, she was exhausted, and it was dark outside. Her stomach rumbled loudly as she dropped her brush into the murky jar of water.

"Feel better?" Celestine asked, handing her a plate with a sandwich on it.

She quickly snatched the sandwich, nearly causing Celestine to drop the plate, and proceeded to devour it.

"Chew, child," Celestine fussed, smiling. She set the plate down on the end table as she walked around the room looking at all of Nideya's work.

Celestine appeared mesmerized by the paintings, inspecting each one carefully. "Are you sure you don't know these people?"

"I'm sure. I ain't never seen them before," Nideya replied. "What does all this mean?"

"You don't know?" she asked bewildered, holding up a painting with a detailed picture of a stern-looking Asian man.

The Asian man had beautiful green eyes, and patches of black scales that had the same green sheen as his long black hair.

"He looks funny, don't he?" Nideya asked, watching the older woman. "I don't get any of it. He's got scales like a lizard. What is he?"

"I'm not sure," she admitted, examining another painting. "But this one looks to be an elemental."

"A what?" She had never heard of such things.

"Elementals are people with power over the elements like water, earth, air, and lightning," Celestine explained.

"Lightning? Why not fire?"

Celestine shook her head. "No one knows, but this is definitely a lightning elemental." She picked up another painting of the Asian man wielding green flames. "Why is the fire green?" she inquired.

Nideya shrugged her shoulders. "I only painted what I saw in my dreams. Do you think Émile might know somethin' about it?"

"I don't know. You'd have to ask him."

"Could they be real people?" Nideya asked curiously. The thought of monsters being real excited her.

"The elemental, most likely, but the lizard man, I can't say for certain." She picked up the painting of the Asian man and the elemental together, surrounded by books. "What's this shadow near them?"

Again, Nideya shrugged.

"I think you should have Emile take you into the city to find out more about these people. These look like visions." Her tone was one of concern.

Nideya knitted her brow in confusion. "But I've never had dream visions before."

"Are you sure of that?" she asked, examining the painting with the Asian man and someone different, another man with scales, as they fought in front of a large house. Fire against water.

"Well, there was the dream about the inkwell," she said, thinking about it, smearing ink on her face as she did so. She looked down at the still-full bottle. "It's funny how I never run out of the stuff."

"Because it's bonded to you. It's in your blood."

"Oh, right."

Celestine put down the painting, then turned to Nideya. "Get some sleep, child. I'll have Emile take you to the city in the morning."

Nideya yawned and stretched. "All right." She could see the worry in her caretaker's eyes. Whatever she saw in the paintings bothered her.

The following morning, Émile readied his pirogue to take them back to the city. Nideya took only the painting with the elemental and the Asian man surrounded by books with her. When she showed Émile the paintings, he lightly touched them and turned his ear to them, as if he were trying to hear what they were saying. He jerked his hand back as if it burned, and started chanting. When he was done, he threw salt at it. His reaction startled her. What was so wrong with her painting? She needed to find out more about the people she painted. She wondered if they were evil, but she did not get that feeling from them. Perhaps she had more to learn about her growing powers.

When they arrived, he took her to Jackson Square and told her to meet him back there in three hours. He told her to be careful of whom she showed the painting to. She agreed and went on her way out of the area.

After the first couple of hours, she was tired and getting hungry. She did not know the name of the bookstore, and no one seemed to be willing to talk to her about it, but she saw the recognition in their eyes. The people in her painting were real.

The fragrant smell of coffee and baked goods filled the air and pulled her by the nose to a small corner bakery. Her stomach complained of its emptiness almost immediately.

"Ooh, sounds like yo stomach's in yo back," came a friendly Cajun voice. "Hey der, Cher! Care to come in for a coffee and some beignets? My mama made 'em fresh."

A tall, lanky boy with rich dark skin came out from behind her. He had a warm, bright smile when he saw her, then he looked down at the painting in her hands.

"Whatcha got der, Cher?" he asked, stepping closer.

She clutched the front of the canvas to her chest protectively, taking a step back.

"It's all right, I don't bite none."

Tentatively, she turned the painting around to show him.

"Dat's a mighty fine paintin' you got der," he said, gently taking it from her.

"Do you know these people? This place?" she asked.

"Sho do! Da place is like magic. Dat der's Kory and Mista Young. Dey run a bookstore not far from here called Bound to Please," he explained. "My name's Lucian. I can take you to it if you like."

She thought about his offer. She wanted to see them, the people that haunted her dreams, but she had no way of knowing if it would be safe. "No, thank you." She took the painting back.

Before she could run off, he caught her arm. "All right, Cher. How about some beignets for da road?"

Again, she took a moment to think, but her stomach answered for her.

"C'mon in. I'll get you somethin' good real quick," he chuckled.

Nideya groaned, but followed the boy named Lucian into Ms. Eve's Beignets and More. Lucian introduced her to his mother, Ms. Eve, and they all chatted while Ms. Eve wrapped up a few beignets and a loaf of sweet bread for her. She graciously took the baked goods, paid with what she had, and then left the shop. She thought of going to Bound to Please on her own, but she had to meet Émile back at Jackson Square. So, her adventure into the unknown would have to wait another day.

Lucian had told her a little about the people in her painting. He had known them for years and said they were good people, though Mr. Young was the grumpy sort. Still, she would talk with Celestine and Émile before she did anything. Until then, she would enjoy the treats she had been given.

CHAPTER 11

It was another balmy afternoon in the Quarter. Andrew had left late that morning to check on patients who could not come into the store. Before that, they had spent the early part of the morning cuddling in bed. It was nice, though Andrew was not overly fond of that sort of affection. But he loved Korlue and knew how much the contact meant to him, so he relented.

Korlue reviewed the stack of books on healing artifacts, going through them to make sure he had ones that would help the stranger. It was then he realized he had never asked the stranger what his name was. He wondered what kind of poison stayed in the body and prevented a wound from healing? How was it that a water elemental or a healer could not remove it? And how did it get into his system in the first place?

His train of thought was derailed when the bell hanging from the front door rang. In walked the stranger, still wearing his hooded cloak and mask. That was something else Korlue wondered about. Why was he hiding? The cloak was understandable; he was a vampire out during the day. But the mask?

"Good afternoon, sir," Korlue smiled, trying not to appear as anxious as he felt.

The smell of the sea and decay preceded him, but the scent of death was not as overpowering as last time. The aura around him was also stronger. He must have fed well recently. Whatever he was doing, it staved off the effects of the poison. Korlue wanted—needed—to know more.

"Good afternoon," came the smooth rasp of his voice. "I hope all is well."

Korlue could not help but blush from the way those ice-blue eyes leered at him from behind the mask. "Yes," he squeaked before clearing his throat. "Yes, all is well."

"Excellent," the stranger said, and Korlue swore he could hear him smiling. "Were you able to find anything that could aid me?"

"I did! But I'm not sure how much of it's true or still around," he explained, trying to pull himself together. He was a former Host, and he did not behave like a flustered woman.

"How do you mean?" the stranger asked, stepping closer to the counter that separated them.

Korlue swallowed hard, shuffling in discomfort. "Well, some of them are really old. Like the Verdant Sigil, for example. I don't think it's been seen in the last couple of centuries." He went through the stack and pulled the book to show him. "And then there's this one." He pulled another from the pile.

"It reads like a fairy tale. I don't even think it's real. I've never heard of the Tideheart Chalice."

The stranger's eyes widened behind his mask, and he gingerly took the dark navy, purplish-blue book from him. It was titled the *Tideheart Chalice and the Oceanborn*. The cover was simple, with silhouettes of coral, fish, and a manta ray. It even had a sea-green gem beneath the title in the shape of a heart, and filigree borders. The stranger held it as if it were a precious heirloom that he had lost. It was odd how he marveled over the thing.

"I'm sure the Bloodmirror Pendant might be better suited to you, seeing as you're a vampire," Korlue said. He found himself feeling oddly jealous of the book.

"I'm not a vampire," he said, gently flipping through the pages with his long, elegant fingers.

"You're not?" Korlue asked, bewildered and suddenly aroused. "But I thought—"

"You were mistaken," he interrupted, still looking at the book. "It's all right; I understand the confusion."

Korlue furrowed his brow. "Then what are you? If you don't mind my asking?"

At that, he looked up from the book. "I'm a demon of sorts and a water elemental."

"What kind of demon?" he asked, narrowing his eyes.

"It's not important." He waved him off, snapping the book shut. "I'll take this book."

"But it's not real, sir. What is your name, by the way?"

"Oh, but it's very real. I had forgotten all about it," he said, fishing a large gold coin from inside his cloak and tossing it on the counter, then turned to leave.

"How can you know that?"

He looked back at Korlue. "I am very old," he replied, going out the door. "And you may call me Jonas. Thank you, Korlue. The offer still stands for you to come see my ship."

Before Korlue could say anything further, the stranger—Jonas—was gone. Korlue was left with more questions than answers. What kind of poison was strong enough to hurt a demon water elemental, and why was he still so attracted to him? He could not even see his face. And how did Jonas know his name? He never gave it to him.

This was all so confusing and mildly irritating. He was at a loss as to what he should do next. Talking to Andrew about it was out of the question since he did not like Jonas or any talk of him. Despite living in the Quarter for so long, his friend space was small. He really only had Lucian as a close friend, and he was not sure talking to a human about non-human things would be all right with him. They barely talked about his powers or Andrew's for that matter.

Korlue sighed in frustration, leaning his elbows on the counter. He really needed to get out and find a community, but he was afraid of people doing him harm because of his relationship with Andrew and for not being human. Andrew was big and strong, fearless in his pursuit of a quieter, less dangerous life. People were afraid of him because of all his scars and his visible scales. They never knew what to make of him.

Running his hand through his long white hair, he thought a trim would be good. Perhaps cutting it all off would be better. Then maybe Madame Delphine would finally admit that he was a man and lay off him.

He rested his head on the counter. His need for a simple, quiet life warred with his desire for one with a little adventure and excitement. Something outside of books.

CHAPTER 12

Andrew was surprisingly tired when he returned home that evening. He had been out for most of the day dealing with his patients. A contented sigh escaped his lips, leaving behind a touch of a smile. It was a simple life, one that he enjoyed. He had his love at his side and two slowly flourishing businesses. It was everything he could have asked for and more than he deserved.

When he stepped through the door to Bound to Please, Korlue was in the process of shutting the store down. He scented the air, then scowled. Mixed with the various smells of human and supernatural patrons, was the scent of the sea and decay touched with a hint of lust. Korlue's lust. The smells were faint, but still lingered. He took a moment to take a calming breath; he knew the stranger would return since Korlue had offered to help him. But despite how much and how well he loved his mate, Korlue was still attracted to the other man. It worried and infuriated him. He did not know what he was doing wrong. Was Korlue bored with him? Was he not enough anymore?

"Andy!" Korlue ran over and embraced him. When he did not respond, he pouted. "What's wrong?"

Andrew looked into his lover's eyes for any sign of discontent and saw nothing but worry. "Nothing is wrong. I am only tired," he lied, forcing a smile.

Korlue made a sound as if he did not believe him, but did not press the issue. "All right, just let me finish closing and we can go have dinner."

"Yes, I would like that," he replied, giving Korlue a light peck on the lips before going to his office at the back of the store. He decided he would not ask about the stranger's visit. If anything had happened, Korlue would tell him. At least he hoped he would.

They had dinner that night at a small bistro close to the store that Korlue had been wanting to try. Andrew was reluctant at first. He did not like being in small spaces with a large group of people, but Korlue insisted they get out now and then. So, he relented. His only thought was of making his mate happy.

Once inside, they were seated at a quaint table near the back. The restaurant was not at capacity, but it was crowded. Apparently, it was a popular destination. Andrew did his best to smile through it.

It had been some time since he had had to be out in such an environment. It was an overload of the senses with the vibrant colors of the murals, the many loud conversations and all the different smells. He tried to distract himself from it all, but it was difficult, especially so close to the full moon. Though he had not gone into a berserker rage since his death, he could still feel the beast crawling beneath his skin.

"Are you all right?" Korlue asked worriedly.

"Yes, I am fine. There is just a lot going on in here, and my senses are overwhelmed with it being so close to the full moon," he replied in a pained tone.

Korlue's bright blue eyes went wide as if he remembered something important. "By the gods! I am so sorry. I forgot about that. We can leave if you want."

Andrew looked at him and smiled. "No, I will be fine. We do not get out often enough," he said, taking his hand. "I wish to be with you in this moment."

Korlue returned his smile and gave his hand a light squeeze. "Tell me about your day; it'll distract you a little."

"My day was busy with sticking needles in people, some of whom did not like me."

Korlue frowned. "What's not to like? You're patient and kind, and so gentle."

"I am also a large Asian man with visible scars and a short temper," he grinned.

Korlue gave him an amused smile that reached his eyes. Andrew thought he was beautiful when he smiled like that.

"Andy, what did you do?"

"I did nothing wrong, but Mr. Beaumont will not be able to feel his tongue for a few days."

"Andrew!" Korlue gasped quietly.

"What? I found him to be irksome," he said matter-of-factly. "Perhaps he will think before he speaks from now on."

Korlue laughed at that. "You're so terrible."

"What of your day?" he asked. "Did anything of note happen?"

Korlue stopped smiling, and Andrew thought he had made a mistake by asking.

"That stranger came back today," he started. "I showed him the books I collected for him, but he was only interested in the one about the Tideheart Chalice. He seems to think it's real."

Andrew grimaced. "I had heard tale of the chalice a long time ago from my former captain."

"Former captain? You were in the military?" Korlue wondered.

"No, I was living on a pirate vessel for nearly a century," he admitted.

Again, Korlue's eyes went wide in surprise. "You were a pirate?" he quietly exclaimed. "Why is this the first I'm hearing of this?"

"Because it never came up," he replied flatly.

Korlue narrowed his eyes at him. "Oh, you are going to tell me all about that later," he fussed lightly.

Andrew smiled warmly at his lover. "I will tell you whatever you want to know."

"Of course you will; you don't have a choice in the matter," he grinned. "But tell me about the chalice. Do you think it's real?"

"It could be. We went looking for it, but never found its location. What made the stranger believe in it?"

Korlue shrugged. "I don't really know, honestly. He just bought the book and left."

Andrew wanted to ask more, but their food arrived, distracting Korlue entirely. For as small as he was, he loved to eat.

They enjoyed their dinner, chatting about Korlue's other customers and about Madame Delphine's absurd prediction about him having a child soon and trying to marry him off to strangers she knew. The prediction irritated Andrew, but it was Madame Delphine. One day, hopefully soon, they would finally be rid of the old crone.

After finishing their meal, they paid and left. Korlue had told him that the stranger's name was Jonas and that he was a water elemental and a demon, though he did not say what kind. It made Andrew happy that Korlue talked to him about it. Though Korlue was reluctant to admit he was still attracted to the other elemental, it eased Andrew's mind that he did not know why. Then it dawned on him.

"I believe this demon elemental is a dying incubus. He most likely has the sickness that kills them," he explained as they went upstairs to their apartment above Bound to Please. "He could also be the one causing all the deaths lately."

"Well, that's scary. Should we turn him in?"

"Do you know where he hides?"

"He did offer to show me his ship again. Maybe we could tell the authorities to look along the docks?" he offered, walking toward the ensuite bathroom.

Andrew furrowed his brow. "When did he make this offer the first time?" He was barely concealing his anger.

"The night I first met him, but I refused and ran away. I thought I told you that," he replied, sticking his head back in the room.

"You did not." He sighed, releasing his anger. "And that is all right," he said, watching him.

Korlue walked over to him and kissed him briefly, cupping his face and rubbing at the light stubble he had grown with his thumbs.

Andrew worked his fingers through the loose braid Korlue had his hair in, freeing and smoothing it across his back. "I love your hair like this. It reminds me of a cloak made of the finest silk," he murmured, his eyes hooded with hunger.

Korlue's hand went to his unbraided hair, combing through part of it as he brought it into his line of sight. "I was thinking of cutting it, actually."

He took hold of Korlue's chin. "Do not cut any of it."

"But it's gotten so long, and washing and drying it takes forever." His breath caught when Andrew's hand lightly wrapped around his throat. "It's just too much to keep up with anymore," he said timidly.

"I will help you care for it," he said. "Do not cut it." When he did not immediately respond, his fingers reflexively tightened around his throat. "Do you agree?"

Korlue's lip trembled. "I agree."

Andrew frowned. "I did not mean to frighten you," he whispered, releasing him. "Please forgive me. I do not know what came over me." But he did. He was a Doll Maker, and Korlue was once a Host, which was similar to Dolls. He was treating his mate like one of his Dolls and not like his partner. It was shameful.

Korlue cupped his face again, holding his head back up to look him in the eyes. "When was the last time you fed?"

He averted his eyes at that. "I am fine," he mumbled. "You need not worry."

Korlue gave him a stern look, then pointed to a large pillar candle sitting on their dresser. "Light it," he commanded.

Andrew sighed. "I cannot." He was feeling a little depleted; it had been more than a few days since he had fed. The last time he did, he had taken too much and hurt his love.

"I knew it!" he proclaimed. "You need to feed, Andy."

He looked him in his crystal blue eyes. "I do not wish to hurt you again."

"Oh, honey. You won't," he said softly. "I trust you."

Andrew's body shuddered against Korlue's, as if the last of his restraint had snapped. He then picked Korlue up, his arms under his rear, and carried him to the bed. The cool surface of the bedding must have tickled the back of his legs, as a surprised 'oh' escaped his lips when Andrew pulled his trousers and underwear off him.

"If you value your shirt," he started, moving to undo his own clothes, "you will remove it."

He watched as Korlue slowly unbuttoned his shirt, but he could no longer wait for him to fumble with what remained of the obstruction. With some effort, Andrew controlled himself just enough to pull the garment over Korlue's head without ripping it. He tossed it to the floor, stopping to admire Korlue's creamy pale skin.

He was thin, but not sickly. In the dim light of their bedroom, he could see the light cording of muscle beneath the surface. He looked as if he had been carved from the finest marble, but he was not. He was made of flesh. Flesh that was aroused and excited for sex. His cock stood tall and erect as it strained and twitched in anticipation, a swollen mass against the flat of his stomach.

His own erection throbbed and ached to be inside of him. He stepped toward his love, shame welling up inside him, as he reached out to caress his cheek.

Korlue held on to his hand and looked up at him. "Don't worry, you won't hurt me this time."

Tired of waiting, Korlue pushed himself off the bed, reaching up for Andrew as he came down. Andrew lifted his lover off the bed, standing with him as Korlue wrapped his legs around his larger body. He realized after a moment that the head of his prick was nestled against the sensitive entrance of Korlue's firm rear. Korlue pulled back slightly to face him, and Andrew could see that the fine blue eyes he had always adored and that were always full of love and curiosity had become dilated and full of need. It made him wonder about the needs of Korlue's vampiric nature that so often went ignored. In their years living together, he had rarely seen the need to feed look so strong in his lover.

Andrew's own fangs ached at the realization of his partner's desire. In the haze of his lust, Korlue loosened his grip around

Andrew's neck and sunk down on him, forcing the large head of Andrew's cock into himself, stretching his delicate hole wide.

Andrew held his weight, not going any further than Korlue had taken him, keeping him locked on the very tip of his erection. He saw the flash of red in Korlue's eyes as he fought for control of his need for blood.

"It would seem that I am not the only one in need of feeding," he murmured. "Is that what you need of me, Kory?" He heard his voice darken as he spoke. "Or did you want me to fuck you first?"

His words seemed to snap Korlue out of his own head. Now there was shame on his lover's face. Andrew had had many partners over the centuries, but none he had wanted to protect the way he had Korlue. He had always been gentle with him, but from the look in his eyes and the potent scent of his lust, he did not need to be treated as if he were a fragile doll. Andrew needed to take him without asking, to be the strong, forceful man he once was. To take control and make him his again.

It had been so long since he had been that man, but he would do whatever Korlue asked of him in that moment, to be what he needed. He would show him with his body. He whisked his lips over his in a momentary, gentle caress before claiming them in a passionate, hungry kiss. In response, Korlue moved his hands to Andrew's shoulders, letting the slight weight of his body force more of Andrew's shaft into his soft tightness. He was so deep that he was sure there was no part of Korlue's body he could not claim with his own.

It was so intimate, the way Korlue gave himself so completely to him. There was no hesitation, only the love and trust they shared.

"Please forgive me." Andrew put his head on Korlue's shoulder briefly before he raised up and brought his open mouth down on the soft, tender space between his neck and shoulder.

Korlue cried out, bucking against him. Andrew grunted at the feel of twin points piercing the skin of his shoulder as they collapsed onto the bed. They remained joined as they took what they needed from each other.

Once he had his fill, Andrew released him, and Korlue did the same. He peered down at his love as he ran a hand up his chest before tweaking a small pink nipple.

"Tell me, what more do you need of me?"

He licked the blood from his full lips before speaking. "Your blood is so hot, I've had my fill of it. Now, I want you to do what you want. Don't hold back."

"Do not ask that of me," he pleaded.

"You asked what I need of you. I need all of you, Andy. Even the dark, scary parts." He kissed him, then looked him in the eyes. "I trust you."

Andrew growled, his body shaking with need and the freeing of what was left of his resistance. "You want my darkness," he snarled, "then take it."

Korlue arched his back as Andrew took him completely, forcing his way through the tight muscles of his ass. He braced himself as Andrew pulled back to thrust back in, harder, faster, making Korlue's back bow again as he cried out. But it was not a cry of pain; he was smiling. Andrew pulled him forcefully to the edge of the bed, jerking himself free of his body. He pulled Korlue up as he steered him to his still-erect phallus.

Wrapping Korlue's hair around his fist, he looked down into his confused eyes. "Take me into your mouth," he commanded. When Korlue stared blankly, Andrew jerked his hair. "This is what I want, Kory. Now open for me."

He wanted Korlue to fully submit to him, and he was not asking. It was a demand. Korlue smiled up at him as his lips parted for him, taking as much of him into his mouth as he could. Andrew was not satisfied with that. He pushed past Korlue's tongue and forced him to take all of him until he gagged.

"Relax your throat, Kory," he ordered.

As he felt the muscles of his throat relax, he began to thrust lightly, winding Korlue's hair tighter around his fist to urge him closer, filling his mouth as deeply as he had his body.

"Yes, very good. Take all of me," he growled.

Korlue moaned around him, taking his own erection into his hands. Andrew watched as his lover stroked himself as he sucked him off. The sight was so erotic that he came without warning. Long, thick ribbons shot into Korlue's mouth, and he greedily drank him dry.

He pulled himself out of Korlue's mouth and forced him back down on the bed. With two fingers, he pushed past the stubborn muscles of his puckered hole, stretching him wide. He fucked him with his fingers, stroking Korlue's cock as he did so.

"Come for me," he demanded as he worked him over. "Now, Kory."

He continued to stroke and finger him, his calloused hand rough against the smooth, sensitive flesh of his prick, his other hand rubbing hard against his insides until Korlue came screaming into his hand. He shook as he ejaculated endlessly onto his stomach and Andrew's hand, his hands in tight fists in the bedding.

Pleasure-blind, Korlue collapsed completely, unable to move, his breathing labored. Andrew moved him further onto the bed, then lay down beside him. He pulled Korlue to him, gently rubbing his back until he calmed.

Korlue opened his eyes to see Andrew grinning down at him. "That was... I don't know what that was."

"Are you satisfied, Qīn'ài de?" he asked, gently wiping sweat-soaked strands from Korlue's flushed face.

Korlue nodded, his eyes closing tiredly as he curled into Andrew.

"Good, so am I," he said, closing his eyes as well. He felt freed, but there was still some concern about how dangerous he was. He did not want to hurt the one person he loved most in the world.

CHAPTER 13

T he dreams always began at the same time—twilight—when the sky was bruised with violet and gold. The bookstore stood alone on a cobbled street, its windows glowing faintly. The sign above the door flickered with lightning runes—symbols only Nideya could read. Inside, the air hummed with static and the scent of old paper. Books whispered as if trying to speak.

The lightning elemental appeared behind the counter, his eyes glowing like storm clouds. His movements were graceful, but his expression was tense. Lightning crackled at his fingertips as he rearranged books that seemed to resist his touch. He spoke in riddles, his voice echoing like thunder.

"The storm remembers what the silence forgets," he said.

Emerging from a back room was the Asian man, his form flickering with scales and smoke. His shadow stretched unnaturally long, curling around shelves like a serpent. He carried a book bound in a scaly hide, its title unreadable. When he opened it, flames leapt from the pages—but they did not burn. He warned Nideya without looking at her.

"The past hunts the future. You must choose who you are before it finds you."

The dream shifted violently. The store began to collapse inward, like a black hole of memory. Books flew from shelves, pages tearing themselves into sigils. Outside, lightning struck repeatedly, forming a circle around the building—an arcane barrier or a trap. Nideya saw herself reflected in a cracked mirror, her eyes glowing, her mouth speaking a prophecy she did not remember learning. Just before she woke, she saw a constellation forming above the bookstore—three stars connected by a jagged line. Then a voice—not the elemental's or the Asian man's—whispered.

"The dream is not a memory. It is a map."

The room was still, save for the frantic thrum of Nideya's heartbeat.

Her body jerked upright, tangled in sweat-damp sheets. Her breath came in shallow bursts, chest rising and falling like a drumbeat. The dream had not faded. It clung to her like smoke, curling around her thoughts, refusing to be forgotten.

She blinked, eyes wide and glassy, staring into the dark. The bookstore. The elemental's storm-lit eyes. The Asian man's serpent shadow. The constellation. The voice.

The dream is not a memory. It is a map.

Her fingers twitched. She did not think—she moved.

She stumbled out of the bed, knocking over a stack of scrolls as she reached for her ink. Her hands found the jar of brushes. She tore a blank canvas from its frame and pinned it to the wall with trembling hands. The moonlight spilled across the floor in fractured silver, illuminating her like a ghost.

Then she began.

Her brush struck the canvas with furious grace. Broad strokes of violet and bruised gold formed the sky. She painted the cobblestone street in jagged lines; the bookstore rising crooked and glowing, its windows bleeding light.

The sign above the door shimmered with lightning runes—symbols she did not know she knew. Her hand moved faster than thought, guided by something ancient and urgent.

Inside the painted shop, she summoned the elemental. Tall, poised, with his eyes like twin topaz. Lightning crackled from his fingertips, illuminating shelves of whispering books. His lips parted mid-riddle.

"The storm remembers what silence forgets."

Next came the Asian man. His form flickered between man and beast—broad shoulders cloaked in shadows, scales glinting beneath his skin. His eyes were bright green, unreadable. He held a book bound in a scaled hide, its pages aflame but untouched by ash.

She painted his warning in the air around him, the words curling like smoke.

"The past hunts the future. You must choose who you are before it finds you."

Around the bookstore, she painted the collapse—the walls folding inward, books flying like birds, pages tearing into sigils. Lightning struck the ground in a perfect circle, enclosing the building in a glowing trap or ward.

Her brush dipped into the ink that had turned silver. She raised it to the top of the canvas.

Three stars. A jagged line. A constellation she had never seen, but knew in her bones. As she painted it, her hand trembled violently. The brush dropped from her fingers, clattering to the floor.

She stepped back, chest heaving, arms streaked with ink. The canvas pulsed with energy. It was not just a painting—it was a message. A warning. A map.

Nideya collapsed to her knees, staring at the painting. Her vision blurred, but the stars remained sharp. She knew with a certainty only oracles possessed that something was coming.

And the bookstore was at the center of it.

The sun had barely risen, casting a pale amber glow over the bayou. Mist clung to the water like a veil, and the cypress trees stood silent, their moss-draped limbs swaying gently in the breeze. The air was thick with the scent of wet earth and jasmine; the only sounds were the distant croak of frogs and the soft ripple of water.

Inside the weathered cabin, Nideya stood before her caretakers, her paintings propped against the wall like doorways to another world.

Celestine, wrapped in a shawl of faded indigo, stared at the canvas with narrowed eyes, a steaming cup of chicory coffee in her hand. The fingers of her free hand traced invisible patterns in the air, her lips pursed in thought.

Émile, tall and quiet, leaned on his cane carved from swamp wood, his blind gaze steady, unreadable. He had felt and heard many things in his years on the water, but the energy pulsing from the canvas made him shift his weight with unease.

The paintings shimmered in the morning light. The crooked bookstore, the elemental's storm-blue eyes, the Asian man's serpent shadow, and the constellation of three stars connected by a jagged silver line.

"I dreamed it again," Nideya said, voice low but firm. "It's not just a dream anymore."

Celestine leaned in, her fingers hovering just above the canvas. "It's a calling," she murmured. "The kind that doesn't wait."

Émile nodded slowly. "You've outgrown this place, Cher. The bayou's quiet now. It doesn't need you like it once did."

Nideya nodded, her voice barely above a whisper. "I feel it in my bones. Somethin's comin'. Somethin' that'll tear through them if I don't go."

Celestine placed a hand on Nideya's shoulder, warm and grounding. "They're standing on the edge of something; you're the only one who sees it coming." She turned her around and took her hand. "You were never meant to stay. You were meant to see. To speak. To warn."

"But what if they're bad people?" she asked, her voice unsure. "The Asian man used to kill people for money, and the elemental was a prostitute."

Celestine smiled warmly. "It is not for you to judge, child. You know what's right in your heart. Trust it."

Nideya grimaced. She had a sour taste in her mouth about the goodness in others after her father kicked her out of his home for having her mother's gift. Only Celestine and Émile accepted her.

Celestine gently cupped her face. "It'll be all right, Nideya. If it doesn't work out, you know you are always welcome here."

"How will I get back here?"

"Oh, we'll know when to come get you," spoke Émile. "You've done your part here. The spirits sleep. But out there..." He tapped the edge of the painting. "They're awake. And they're waiting."

Nideya packed lightly—her brushes, her paints, the ink, and a few canvases. She also packed the paintings she had done the night before. She hugged Celestine tightly, breathing in the scent of herbs and coffee. Émile waited by the dock, his pirogue bobbing gently in the water.

"I'll come back," Nideya said, though she was not sure it was true.

Celestine smiled, sad and proud. "You'll go where you're needed."

Émile helped her into the boat, then pushed off with a practiced shove. As the pirogue glided silently through the water, the mist parted like a curtain, revealing the winding path back to the city. Cypress trees loomed like sentinels, and the water whispered secrets beneath the boat.

Neither of them spoke. Émile rowed with practiced ease, his vacant eyes on the horizon. Nideya sat at the bow, her paintings rolled and tucked beside her, her gaze fixed ahead.

The city emerged from the mist like a dream remembered—iron balconies dripping with vines, cobblestone streets slick from the previous night's rain, the scent of pralines and river water in the air.

They docked near the Quarter, where the buildings leaned close like gossiping old friends, and Émile helped her ashore. He did not say goodbye, just tipped his hat and vanished into the mist.

Nideya stood alone, her paintings under her arm, her heart heavy with purpose.

She found the bookstore easily. Just as in her dream, only it was not crooked, but its windows glowed faintly. The sign above the door shimmered with lightning runes only she could see and read.

She did not enter.

Instead, she crossed the street and settled onto a wrought-iron bench beneath a flickering gas lamp. The paintings rested beside her, wrapped and silent.

Inside, she saw movement.

The elemental, radiant and restless, rearranged books with a flick of his fingers. His long white hair sparked faintly, and his eyes scanned the shelves as if he were searching for something he could not name.

The scaly Asian man emerged from the back, broad and brooding, with a book in his hand.

They looked ordinary. Mortal. Fragile. But Nideya knew better. She watched them, her eyes sharp, her heart a storm of doubt and duty.

"Let's see," she whispered, "if you're worth saving."

CHAPTER 14

K orlue searched his entire store for any books he might have had on the Tideheart Chalice and the Oceanborn. He looked for anything that referenced either one and found very little outside of what he had already sold. He had never been one to chase legends. Pragmatism usually tempered his curiosity, but something about the chalice gnawed at him.

Dust motes danced in shafts of light filtering through the windows. He pulled books from every corner—old tomes, forgotten journals, even water-damaged scrolls he had never bothered to catalog. His fingers moved with urgency, flipping pages, scanning margins for any mention of the Oceanborn or their enigmatic Tidemother.

Most texts were silent on the matter. A few referenced ancient maritime cults, but none directly named the chalice. The only substantial mention remained in the book he had sold to Jonas—a volume he now regretted parting with. It concerned him that Jonas might be the incubus doing the killings, but it explained why he covered himself and refused to tell Korlue what he was. He wondered if he was meant to be Jonas' next victim the night they danced.

He was able to piece together fragments of what he was looking for between helping customers. It was mostly what he had already known from reading the first book, but he discovered that water elementals and demons bore a resonance with the chalice, drawn to it like tides to the moon.

Korlue scribbled notes furiously. If the chalice was real, it was not just a relic—it was a beacon. And if Jonas had it, or was close to finding it, he could likely cure himself of the poison that was slowly killing him. Somehow, that did not sit well with Korlue. Jonas was a dangerous killer, and he could not be trusted with the healing powers of the chalice. Though he did not know him well enough to make that assessment, Jonas was probably only killing to stay alive. That was no excuse for the behavior, but Korlue understood it. Perhaps it was not his intention to kill at all.

As he worked, he noticed a young girl lingering outside the store. She could not have been more than twelve or thirteen, dressed in worn clothes, with a satchel of paintbrushes and canvas paper rolled and tucked under her arm. Her eyes were sharp—watching, not wandering. She had shoulder-length wavy dark-brown hair. Though they looked wary, she had warm golden-brown eyes.

She was short and adorable, and clearly of mixed race with her light brown skin. He saw splotches of ink and paint on her face and hands. Curious, he stepped outside to greet her.

"You don't have to be outside in this sticky heat," he said, smiling.

She just stood there, staring wide-eyed, as if she had been caught doing something wrong.

"Why don't you come in? I'd love to see your paintings," he tried.

At that, she slowly started to back away.

"Oh, please don't be scared," he said. "You're welcome to come in and paint, if you'd like. I'd gladly get you some food, too."

She stood still for a moment, holding her loudly growling belly. "I don't trade with strangers," she said, her voice barely above a whisper. Then she turned and bolted down the alley, her footsteps echoing in the distance.

In her haste, she dropped one of her paintings. He picked it up and unfurled it. What he saw shocked him, and he nearly dropped it. She had painted a fancy cup carved from obsidian with veins of coral that glowed faintly. It sat on a gray pedestal surrounded by shelves of different items he could not make out, but did not seem important. What stood out most was the bright sea-green gemstone in the shape of a heart centered on the cup. It was the Tideheart Chalice. He could feel it. It was just as described.

How did this girl know about the chalice? What did this mean? Was she sent by Jonas to deliver a message? Korlue stood there for a moment, watching the empty street with the painting at his side. He felt the weight of the day and so much more pressing on him—the unanswered questions, the girl's wary gaze, the silence of his books. Absentmindedly, he stroked his long braid, then looked at it. It had been long his whole life. He only kept it long because it was what others wanted.

He needed clarity. A reset. To do what he wanted.

So, he locked up the store, then walked to the barber down the street, a small place with cracked leather chairs. The bell above the shop door jingled with a tired chime as Korlue stepped inside. The place smelled of sandalwood, old leather, and the faint metallic tang of scissors. It was quiet—just the hum of clippers and the low murmur of a radio playing some forgotten jazz tune.

The barber, an older man with silver temples and sleeves rolled up to the elbow, looked up from his chair. "You're late," he said, not unkindly. "Or early. Depends on how you measure time."

Korlue smirked. "I measure it in how long it takes for me to stop looking like a woman."

He settled into a cracked leather chair, its cushion sighing beneath him. The mirror in front of him was slightly fogged, as if reluctant to show him clearly. He stared at his reflection—his hair was so long, and he knew how much it meant to his mate, but the weight of it was getting to be too much.

The old barber draped a faded cape over him, the fabric smelling faintly of mint and talc. Scissors clicked rhythmically, snipping away strands like shedding old thoughts. Korlue closed his eyes, letting the sound lull him into a rare moment of stillness.

"You've got something on your mind," the barber said, combing through the remaining locks. "Something heavy."

Korlue hesitated. "Ever chase something so hard you start to wonder if it's chasing you back?"

The barber chuckled. "Only every time I fall in love."

As the hair fell to the floor, Korlue imagined each strand as a piece of doubt, a fragment of the man who dismissed his own needs and wants. Andrew, the store, the surrounding strangeness—all of it fit neatly into his world. But maybe his world needed reshaping.

The barber leaned in, trimming the edges with precision. "You look like someone about to make a decision."

"I think I already did," Korlue murmured.

He looked in the mirror again. The man staring back was cleaner, sharper—but still haunted. He paid in silence, leaving a generous tip and a quiet thank you.

Outside, the wind had picked up, carrying the scent of rain and salt. Korlue ran a hand through his shorter hair and felt lighter—not just in appearance, but in purpose. He turned toward the alley where the girl had vanished, the memory of her wary eyes still fresh. Something told him she had not run far.

CHAPTER 15

T he slow, mournful wail of a trumpet drifted down the street, weaving through the humid air like a ghost. A brass band led the funeral procession, their instruments gleaming like polished bones in the late summer sun, playing a dirge that clung to the cobblestones. Behind them, mourners in black walked solemnly, some weeping, others silent. At the center of it all was the casket—lacquered mahogany, carried by six men in white gloves. The dead man inside had been a husk, found smiling, eyes wide open, lips curled in eerie bliss.

Korlue watched from the bookstore window, his arms folded tightly across his chest. The glass fogged slightly from his breath. He had seen too many of these processions lately. Too many husks with the same unnatural grin.

Behind him, Andrew moved through the stacks, shelving books with quiet precision. He had no patients that day and had offered to help with the new shipment of books. His back was straight, his movements smooth, almost rehearsed. Korlue did not need to see his face to know he was avoiding the conversation.

"There goes another one," Korlue said, his voice low.

Andrew did not respond.

"Another husk," he added, turning from the window. "We can't keep pretending this isn't happening."

Andrew slid a book into place. "We are not pretending. We are staying out of it."

Korlue stepped forward, the scent of old paper and ink wrapping around him like a shroud. "We can't ignore this."

"We are not ignoring it," Andrew said. "We are surviving."

Korlue's jaw tightened. "You know what this is. You know what he is."

Andrew finally looked up, his green eyes calm and unreadable. "And I know what I am."

That stopped Korlue cold. Andrew rarely spoke of his past, but it hung between them like a shadow. Assassin. Cleaner. Ghost. He had walked away from that life a long time ago, burying it beneath stacks of books and quiet mornings. But it was still there, just beneath the surface. When he was Raesh, he was lethal. Dangerous. Even during his time with the circus, he had killed needlessly. He had worked hard to escape that part of himself. Finding love had helped a great deal.

"I'm not asking you to be that man again," Korlue murmured. "I'm asking you to help stop a killer."

Andrew looked at him, and for a moment, Korlue saw a flicker of something deep and old behind his eyes. Not fear. Never fear. Andrew feared almost nothing. But he feared becoming what he used to be and losing his mate.

"I have spent the last four years trying to forget what I did," he said. "Trying to build something quiet. Something human."

"And you think letting people die is human?"

Andrew's gaze dropped to Korlue's hair—short now, cropped just below his ears. The long strands Andrew used to run his fingers through were gone. Korlue saw the flicker of hurt in his eyes, even if he tried to hide it.

"You said you would not cut it," Andrew murmured.

"I needed a change."

"You agreed," he argued.

"I changed my mind," he snapped.

Andrew stepped back. The tension between them was as thick as molasses. "You did not just change your hair. You changed the way you look at me."

Korlue swallowed hard. "I'm scared, Andy. Jonas is still out there. And he's hurting people."

Andrew leaned against the bookshelf, rubbing his temples. "You believe I am afraid?"

"No," Korlue said. "I think you're not scared at all. And that's what terrifies me."

Outside, the procession turned the corner, the music fading into the distance. The silence that followed was heavy, as if the city itself was holding its breath.

"I want to stop watching people die with smiles on their faces," Korlue said after a moment. "I'm tired of doing nothing when I know things."

Andrew sighed, his shoulders sagging. "You are not going to let this go, are you?"

"No," he said, with a glimmer of hope and confidence in his tone. "And neither should you."

"He has what he needs to find what he is looking for. He will leave soon."

"When?" Korlue demanded. "After he's taken out half the city?"

Andrew gave him an exasperated look. "I do not wish to argue with you. I believe we should stay out of it," he started. "He will eventually have to leave before he is discovered."

"You really don't care about anyone, do you?" Korlue asked softly.

"I care about you," he countered. "That is enough. I do not wish for the attention helping will bring."

Korlue made a disgusted sound, staring at his lover in disbelief. When Andrew reached for him, he jerked away, discharging a bolt at him. Slowly, he backed away toward the door.

"Kory, please. You must understand," Andrew pleaded.

It was the first time Korlue had seen fear in his eyes since he was taken four years ago.

"I need to go," Korlue said, his voice barely above a whisper. Then he was out the door, with Andrew shouting his name.

CHAPTER 16

T he morning rays of sunlight trickled through the sliver between the curtains, rousing him from his slumber. Andrew was usually an early riser, but he had stayed up waiting for Korlue. Korlue had returned late that evening, leaving Andrew to close the store alone. When he finally stumbled back in, he was drunk and surly. Which was out of character for him, as he did not drink. Once again, Korlue refused Andrew's touch, and passed out near the edge of his side of the bed.

As Andrew got up, he reached over to Korlue's side of the bed. It was cold, as if he did not sleep there at all. It had been the night of the new moon, so he did not notice when Korlue left. He was always so tired and weak during the new moon.

Andrew sighed as he got out of bed. It did not surprise him that he woke up alone. He thought of going after Korlue that night, but decided it was best to give him space.

They had never fought like this before. And Andrew thought they were back in a good place since Korlue's night out when he met the incubus, but he was wrong. He would have to make things right with his mate using something other than a sound fucking. Relationships were not his strong suit, but he knew others who had strong ones.

He went downstairs to the store to find Korlue hard at work sorting and shelving books. And ignoring him. When he reached for his shoulder, Korlue moved away, refusing to even look at him. He just kept working.

With his head held low, Andrew whispered, "I am sorry." He wrote a brief note saying he would be out for most of the day visiting an old friend and would be back before closing. After that, he left.

Andrew traveled a short distance out of New Orleans to the old plot of land the Cirque du Arcane once called home. With very few survivors left, the troop disbanded and went their separate ways. He had no use for the land, so he sold it to a pack of werewolves he had known that needed a new home. Li Wei, the grandson of Su Yang, the physician of the Pale Emperor and Andrew's old mentor, led the pack.

After Andrew had left the crew of the Pale Emperor to strike out on his own, he kept tabs on the old wolf. Su Yang retired soon after Andrew left and went back to his family. He had died some years later under mysterious circumstances. Andrew never found out what happened to him, but he kept watch over his family ever since.

The sun was hiding behind the cypress trees, bleeding yellow into the swamp mist. Cicadas buzzed in the heavy air, and the scent of damp earth and honeysuckle clung to everything. Andrew stood at the edge of the property he had once owned, wolves young and old milling about. The house Liwei had built stood proud and simple—whitewashed wood, a wraparound porch, and a rocking chair that creaked with the breeze. He had not meant to come. But after the fight with Korlue, he had needed somewhere quiet. Somewhere neutral.

The screen door creaked open.

Liwei stepped out, tall and broad-shouldered, his amber eyes gleaming with quiet strength. His dark hair was tied back, his sleeves rolled to his elbows, a smear of flour on his forearm. His gaze was steady, calm. He was young still, but already carried the weight of a pack leader with calm authority and quiet grace.

"Well," Liwei said, wiping his hands on a towel. "You look like you've been dragged through the bayou backwards."

Andrew gave a tired smile. "Feels about right."

Liwei did not move. "You want tea or silence."

"Tea," Andrew replied, though he still hated it. But he put up with it for Korlue's sake. "But I will take both."

Inside the house was warm and simple. A cast-iron skillet rested on the stove, and the scent of rosemary and cornbread lingered in the air. Liwei poured sweet tea into two mason jars and handed one over without ceremony.

"You still watching us?" Liwei asked.

Andrew took the jar, eyes downcast. "Not like before. Just... keeping tabs. I owed Su Yang. Still do."

Andrew sat at the kitchen table, the wood worn smooth by time. He did not speak again right away.

Liwei finally broke the quiet, taking the seat across from him. "You and Korlue. What happened?"

Andrew stared into his glass of over-sugared brown water. "We disagreed."

Liwei raised a brow. "That's vague."

Andrew hesitated. "There is someone dangerous. Someone hurting people. Korlue wants to help stop them. I do not."

Liwei leaned back in his chair, arms crossed. "Why not?"

"Because it is not my fight," he replied, his voice low.

Liwei narrowed his eyes. "You sure?"

Andrew looked up. "I do not know this man. Korlue does. Not well, but enough to feel responsible. He believes I am being a coward."

Liwei did not answer right away. He got up and walked to the window, looking out at the land—the slow-moving water, the trees heavy with moss. "You sold this place because you said it needed someone who'd care for it. Someone who'd listen to it."

Andrew nodded.

Liwei turned back to him. "So, listen. If someone's hurting people, and you can help stop it, it's your fight. Whether or not you know them."

Andrew's jaw tightened. "It is not that simple."

"It never is," Liwei said, his voice soft. "But Korlue's not angry because you disagreed. He's angry because you didn't stand beside him. You left him to carry it alone."

Andrew looked down. "I did not mean to."

Liwei sat back down, folding his hands. "Then go tell him that. And mean it."

The cicadas outside sang louder, and the wind stirred the moss like breath through lace.

Liwei did not know the details. He did not know about the incubus or the bodies or the way Korlue had looked at him as if he did not recognize him anymore. But he knew the shape of guilt. And he knew what it meant to choose silence over action.

"You don't have to fix it," Liwei spoke. "But you do have to show up."

Andrew nodded slowly, the weight of the words settling deep. "Thank you."

Liwei smiled faintly. "Don't thank me yet. Go earn it."

"I will."

"But first," he started. "Come run with me."

Andrew raised a confused brow. "Are you certain?"

Liwei glanced at him. "You need it."

The sun was high, filtering through the canopy in golden shafts that danced across the forest floor. The air was warm and thick with the scent of pine, river water, and the faint sweetness of blooming jasmine.

Andrew stood at the edge of the woods behind Liwei's house, rolling his shoulders as he eyed the trail ahead.

He looked down at his hands—steady now, but he could feel the pressure building beneath his skin. The dragon within him was old, coiled and patient. But the wolf was newer, rawer, and harder to control. The bite had come several decades ago, from a werewolf whose name he no longer spoke. It had not killed him. It had changed him. He was a dragon that obeyed the call of the moon.

Liwei had been helping him manage the transformations for years now. Not with spells or potions, but with rhythm. With instinct. And with trust.

"Let's go," Liwei said, already shifting as he removed his clothes.

His body rippled, bones reshaping with fluid grace. Fur spread across his skin like wildfire, and in seconds, the wolf stood tall and lean, eyes gleaming gold.

Andrew closed his eyes as he removed the last of his clothes, and let go.

The change was slower for him—less natural. His body stretched, cracked, and reshaped. Scales shimmered briefly across his skin before giving way to fur. His limbs elongated, claws forming, breath deepening. The dragon did not vanish—

it folded back, watching. The wolf came forward, snarling softly.

Liwei took off first, a blur of motion through the trees. Andrew followed, his gait heavier, more chaotic, but gaining rhythm with each stride. The forest opened around them, branches parting as if they remembered the shape of their bodies.

They ran.

Through the pines, over roots and fallen logs, past the slow-moving water that reflected their bodies. The wind rushed past, carrying the scent of deer, of wet stones, of old magic. Andrew's mind quieted. The guilt, the fight with Korlue, the incubus—it all fell away beneath the pounding of his paws.

Liwei slowed near a bend in the trail, shifting back with a smooth exhale. Andrew followed, his hair damp with sweat, breath ragged.

They sat on a fallen log, sunlight warming their backs.

"You're holding the shift better," Liwei said, getting up to splash the cool river water on his face.

Andrew did the same. "It still feels like I am borrowing someone else's skin."

Liwei shrugged. "You're not though. You're just learning to wear it."

Andrew looked out at the trees. "I have been running from things for a long time now."

Liwei nodded. "And now you're running toward something."

"Do you ever feel like you are more than one thing?"

Liwei smiled wryly. "I'm a leader. A mate. A father. A wolf. Some days I'm all of them. Some days I'm none. But I run. That's what keeps me whole." He sat down on the grass.

Andrew lay down on the grass, staring at the sky. "Korlue believes I do not know how to be part of something."

Liwei did not answer immediately. "You do. You just forget. You've lived too long in your own shadow."

"You think I should help?" Andrew asked, turning his head.

Liwei met his gaze. "I think you should stop hiding. From your mate. From yourself. And from the part of you that wants to do the right thing."

The wind stirred the trees, and somewhere in the distance, a bird called.

Andrew closed his eyes. "I will try."

Liwei stood, stretching. "Good. Now come on. You owe me a race back."

Andrew grinned, fangs flashing.

They ran again, faster this time, the forest alive around them. Two shapes moving through the late afternoon sun—one born of fire, one born of moonlight—learning, slowly, how to run side by side. The sun was beginning to dip, casting long shadows across the path. Andrew ran harder, breath steady, heart pounding—not just from the run, but from the decision forming in his chest.

He would make it back before the store closed. And this time, he would not stay silent.

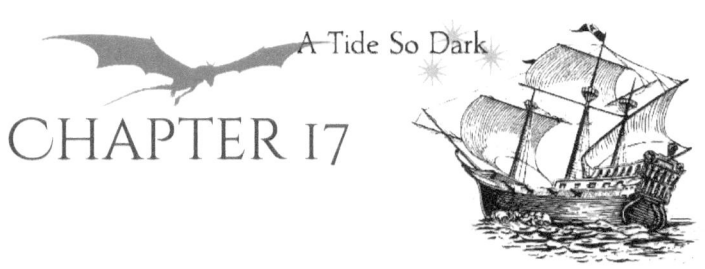

CHAPTER 17

Nideya came to slowly, her senses swimming through a fog of heat and color. The world felt distant, like she was still inside the fever dream that had gripped her for days. Her body ached, her throat was dry, and her skin was clammy with sweat. Her head throbbed, a dull ache behind her eyes, and her limbs felt like they had been stitched together with lead. She blinked against the soft light, trying to orient herself.

The world came back in fragments—light slanting through dusty windows, the scent of old paper and dried herbs, the muffled creak of footsteps. She was lying on a warm couch—in the back of the bookstore, she realized, with its walls lined with crooked shelves.

Two figures hovered nearby.

One was a boy, who looked around her age, with deep brown skin and a wary expression. He wore suspenders over a rumpled shirt, and his eyes flickered between her and something behind her.

The other was a man—though at first glance, Nideya had thought him a woman. He was tall and slight, with short white hair and a face so finely drawn it looked carved from porcelain. His clothes were neat, pressed, but his posture was tense.

She vaguely remembered the boy, Lucian, from when she visited his mother's bakery. But she did not know the white-haired man's name. Not yet. But she had seen him before—in her visions. Though his hair was longer then. He had appeared in flashes, standing in the doorway of his store, watching the street as if he were waiting for something to go wrong. She had been watching him and the store since she had left the bayou.

And now, here he was, watching her.

"Je suis au l'moure," the boy said, his voice quiet but edged with curiosity. "You're awake."

Nideya tried to sit up, but the motion sent a wave of dizziness crashing through her. She clutched the arm of the couch and nodded.

"Ya passed out," Lucian started. "We found ya across da street... wit dat."

He gestured toward the canvas propped up against the wall behind her. Nideya's breath caught. The painting. Her fevered vision, rendered in frantic strokes and bleeding color—a violent clash between two figures, one of them unmistakably the Asian man from her visions, his face twisted in fury, his hands raised in defense or attack. The other figure was cloaked in shadow, faceless, featureless, a smear of darkness that seemed to pulse with menace. Like it had been painted with ink and nightmares.

"I-I ain't mean to scare anyone," she said, her voice hoarse. "I just been watchin' the store for a little while. I like to paint. Sometimes things just come to me, and I have to get them out."

Lucian studied her as if trying to decide whether she was dangerous or just strange. "I remember ya," he said finally. "Ya came by my mama's bakery last week. Asked about the bookstore. I always remember a pretty girl."

Nideya flushed. "I ain't mean nothin' by it. I just wanted to know if it was real."

The man stepped closer, his arms folded. "I've seen you, too. Watching the shop. You ran from me."

"I'm sorry," she said quietly. "I ain't mean to cause trouble."

He glanced back at the painting. "What is this?"

She looked at the painting again, her stomach twisting. It felt like a warning. Or a memory that had not happened yet. "I-I just paint," she replied. "I don't mean nothin' by it."

The man's expression darkened. "The person fighting Andrew... their face is hidden."

"I couldn't see it," Nideya whispered. "It was just shadows. But it feels... important."

The man glanced at the boy. "Luc, go check the front. Make sure no one's coming."

Lucian nodded and slipped out, leaving Nideya with the white-haired man.

"Does Andrew know about this?" he asked.

"No," Nideya said quickly. "Please don't tell him. I don't want him to think I'm spyin' or somethin'. I just... I needed to paint it."

He studied her for a long moment. Then he sighed and stepped back. "Fine. For now. Where do you live?"

She held her head low, avoiding his gaze. She thought about lying but decided not to. "I ain't got no place to stay anymore. My mama died, and my daddy got a new family and don't want me."

The man frowned. "Well, you can stay here for now. You're sick and need proper food and rest."

Nideya nodded, clutching the blanket around her shoulders. Her eyes drifted back to the painting. The shadows around the second figure seemed deeper now, more deliberate. She did not know who it was. But she had a feeling she would. And soon.

CHAPTER 18

The ship groaned beneath the weight of its own secrets, its timbers swollen with river rot. Lanterns swung low, casting a jaundiced light across the warped deck boards, and the Mississippi's breath curled around the hull like a warning. Below deck, in the captain's quarters, Jonas sat hunched over a leather-bound tome, its pages brittle with age and ink that pulsed faintly under his touch.

He was gaunt now—more shadow than man. The silk of his shirt clung to his chest, damp with sweat, and his once-gilded voice had thinned to a rasp. Yet the crew still feared him. Revered him. They knew what he was, even if they dared not speak it aloud.

An incubus nearing the end.

But he was more than that. He was also a water elemental. One with mastery over blood. That was what they truly feared. He had systematically eliminated the entire former crew of the ship, the former captain included. Even though the poison was slowly killing him, he was still a force to be reckoned with.

The door creaked open. A crewman entered, his eyes lowered, dragging behind him a trembling figure—a young man, bound at the wrists, his pulse fluttering visibly at his throat.

Jonas did not look up. "Leave him," he said, his voice like velvet fraying at the edges.

The crewman obeyed, retreating as if from a shrine. The door shut, and silence bloomed.

Jonas turned a page. The book he had bought from Korlue days ago—Korlue with his ink-stained fingers and eyes like rare topaz. Korlue, who had looked so confused when he handed over the volume, unable to understand what Jonas was truly seeking.

The Tidevault. The chalice. Salvation.

His fingers trembled as he traced a passage. "Where the sea forgets its name, beneath the drowned cathedral, the chalice waits."

He closed his eyes. Jonas could still smell Korlue—cedarwood and old paper. He wanted him. Not just his knowledge, not just his vitality. He wanted the man. Wanted to possess him, to keep him close as the hunger grew unbearable.

He went back to his reading. The book was more than just a map. It was a tether. Every glyph, every passage, pulled him back to that night.

The jazz club had a name he did not care to remember—it had just a red door. Inside, it pulsed with jazz and sweat—slick bodies, the air thick with gin and longing. The walls were velvet-draped, the lighting low and golden, like candlelight caught in amber. Korlue had arrived in black clothes and defiance, fresh from a fight with his lover. He had wanted danger. He had wanted a distraction.

Jonas had fed well that day, and he had come looking for Korlue.

He found him. And though it took a little convincing, they danced. Not a waltz—a slow, aching sway, bodies close, breath mingling. His hand on Korlue's waist like it belonged there. Korlue's pulse raced. Jonas had wanted him then. Not just his body. His mind. His soul. And then Jonas whispered something—intimate—into Korlue's ear. Then, just as he leaned in to claim him, Korlue pulled away—eyes wide, frightened, guilty—and fled into the crowd.

Jonas had not chased him. He did not need to. His spies were already watching the bookstore. Watching Korlue.

Back aboard his ship, Jonas closed the book and stared into the candle's flame. He remembered the way Korlue trembled—not from fear, but from recognition. Jonas had tasted something eternal in that moment. And he would taste it again.

The bound man whimpered.

Jonas rose slowly, the light catching the unnatural gleam in his eyes. His movements were deliberate, almost reverent, as he approached the captive. The man shrank back, wrists straining against the rope, eyes wide with terror—but beneath the fear, Jonas could smell it. Vitality. Youth. The kind of life that burned hot and fast.

"Shhh," he whispered, brushing a strand of hair from the man's damp forehead. "It won't take long."

His voice was velvet and ruin. The man trembled, tears streaking his cheeks, but Jonas was not cruel in that moment. He did not need pain. He needed essence. The soul's heat. The pulse of memory and desire that lived just beneath the skin. He gently pressed his lips to the captive's, his palm on the man's chest, fingers splayed over the heart. The skin beneath his touch flushed, then paled. He released him from his kiss, his mouth hovering about his. A blue shimmer left the captive's lips—a stream, faint, flickering like water in candlelight. The man gasped, his back arching, as Jonas began to draw.

It was not blood. It was something deeper. Vitality. Emotion.

The captive's breath hitched, his eyes rolling back as Jonas fed—not with fangs, but with hunger older than language. He devoured the man's joy, his regrets, the echo of a mother's lullaby, the memory of a first kiss. All of it flowed into Jonas, warming his bones, sharpening his senses.

But it was not enough. Not anymore.

He could feel the hollowness still gnawing at him, the rot in his veins, the ticking clock of his life. The man's skin turned gray and ashen, with a giddy smile on his face. Nothing left but a husk of what used to be. Jonas backed away, swaying slightly, the candlelight painting shadows across his face.

He wiped his mouth, though there was no blood. Only longing. Only Korlue. He turned back to the book, hands trembling, eyes burning. The words shimmered faintly, as if mocking him. The chalice was out there. Somewhere beneath the drowned cathedral, where the sea forgets its name. He would find it.

And Korlue... Korlue would be his. One way or another.

CHAPTER 19

T he sun had dipped low by the time he had returned home, casting the sky in deep shades of violet and orange. Korlue had already locked up the store, so he had to go to the side entrance of their home. Andrew did his best to take Liwei's words to heart, but it was easier said than done. He had no interest in going after the incubus, though he wanted him dead. He enticed Korlue, and he found that to be vexing. However, he wanted to do right by his mate, even if he was not sure of his immortality.

Andrew still healed fast, and he still had his strength and durability, but had never tested whether his immortality was intact after all this time. The goddess who resurrected him made changes and never said whether his immortality remained. While he was not afraid of death, he feared leaving Korlue behind. He did not want to put him through that again. Though, now that he thought about it, Korlue had not mourned him long. He had gone back to his old life without issue. What if he did not actually love him? What if he was just a means to free Korlue from a life of prostitution?

No, he could not allow himself to think like that. Korlue loved him, and the last four years, though quiet, were wonderful. At least it was for him. Perhaps Liwei was right. He needed to listen to Korlue. He needed to listen to what his mate wanted and fulfill it to the best of his ability.

Andrew let out a heavy sigh as he looked at the door, his hand around the knob. There would be no more hiding. No more running away. He straightened his back, looking ahead. Things would be made right tonight.

The apartment was dim, lit only by the amber glow of the kitchen lamp. The windows were open, but the breeze had long since abandoned the city. Outside, a streetcar rattled past, its bell a distant echo. The scent of chicory coffee and river damp clung to the walls, mingling with the faint aroma of thyme and a simmering broth.

Andrew stepped through the door, sweat clinging to the back of his neck. His shirt was damp from the run and the August heat, his boots dusty from the cracked sidewalks and humid alleys. He paused in the stairwell, listening as he removed his boots.

Voices. One familiar. One new.

He climbed the stairs slowly, each creak of the wood a reminder of the tension still lingering between him and Korlue. The fight had not been loud, but it left a mark—like a bruise beneath the skin.

He reached the kitchen doorway and stopped. The smell of thyme was stronger, along with something metallic—blood, maybe—faint but present.

Korlue stood at the counter, slicing root vegetables with methodical precision. His sleeves were rolled to the elbows, and his hair was damp, curling at the nape of his neck. Across the room, curled in the armchair by the hearth, sat a young girl.

She looked to be no more than twelve or thirteen. Thin, dark-skinned, with tightly braided hair and a shawl draped over her shoulders despite the heat. Her fingers were stained with streaks of blue and ochre. A canvas rested on her lap, half-covered in swirls of color—storm clouds, a ship, something broken beneath the waves. She did not look up when Andrew entered. She was painting with her fingers, slow and deliberate, as if each stroke mattered more than breath.

Andrew's jaw tightened as his gaze lingered on the painting.

Korlue glanced over his shoulder. "You're back."

Andrew nodded. "Who is she?"

"Nideya," Korlue said. "Luc and I found her collapsed across the street. She was burning up. Barely conscious."

His eyes stayed on the girl as he stepped into the room, the floorboards groaning beneath him. "She is sick?"

"Starved. Exhausted. Something else, maybe. She hasn't said much after we found her." Korlue turned back to the cutting board. "She's staying here. Just for a few nights."

Andrew stepped in further, the warmth of the kitchen brushing against his skin like a memory he did not want. "Is that safe?"

Korlue's knife paused mid-slice. "She's a child."

Andrew did not answer. He did not like children. Never had. They were too unpredictable, too fragile, too loud. But he said nothing. Because Korlue knew that. And because tonight, he did not want to be the one who broke something.

"She paints," Korlue said, his voice quieter. "Hasn't stopped since she woke up. She doesn't speak much, but she watches everything."

Andrew glanced at the canvas. The ship in the painting looked eerily familiar. His stomach turned.

"She's gifted," Korlue added. "I don't know how, but... there's something in her work. Like she's seeing something we're not."

Andrew's voice was low. "She has magic. Something strange with her blood."

Korlue furrowed his brow. He had stopped cutting again. "She's been on the streets for a while from the look of her."

"You know how I feel about children," he said, his voice even.

"I do," Korlue replied. "But I'm not going to let her live outside in this heat while she's sick."

Andrew nodded slowly. "I did not say you were wrong."

Korlue's expression did not soften. "Good, because I didn't ask."

A silence settled between them, thick with unspoken things.

Andrew cleared his throat. "Can we talk? Just us?"

Korlue looked at Nideya, who had paused mid-stroke, her dark eyes flickering up for the first time.

"Sweetheart," Korlue said gently, "can you finish that in the sitting room?"

Nideya nodded and rose, gathering her canvas, paints, and a strange bottle of color-shifting ink. She moved past Andrew without a word, her presence oddly weightless, as if she did not quite belong to the room.

When she was gone, Andrew leaned against the counter. "I came to make things right."

Korlue did not speak... or release the knife in his hand.

"I should have listened to you," he said. "I let my fear speak louder than my heart. I let it tell me what you wanted was dangerous. That loving you was dangerous."

Korlue's voice was quiet. "You think this is about love?"

Andrew stepped closer. "I believe everything is."

Korlue looked away, then began to put the vegetables he had been cutting into the simmering pot. "She reminds me of me. When I was her age. Alone. Sick. No one wanted me."

"I want you," he said softly.

Korlue's eyes met his, and for a moment, the walls cracked.

"I hate that I made you feel alone. I do not want to lose you."

"You almost did."

Andrew swallowed. "I want to help. With her. With this. I want to be the man you see in me. The man you fell in love with."

Korlue's eyes softened, but his voice remained firm. "Then stop hesitating. Stop weighing every decision like it's a transaction. We can be a part of our community without our pasts getting in the way. We can help others."

Andrew nodded. "I understand. I will do better."

Korlue turned back to the stove, ladling soup into the bowl. "Then start by bringing her this."

Andrew took the bowl, the heat seeping into his hands. He turned toward the sitting room, his heart heavy but steadier than it had been.

Behind him, Korlue stirred the pot, the quiet rhythm of care resuming—one life at a time.

Andrew stepped into the sitting room, bowl in hand, the scent of thyme and bone broth rising with the steam. The room was dimly lit by a single oil lamp on the side table, its flame flickering against the walls like a heartbeat.

Nideya sat cross-legged on the floor, her canvas propped against the arm of the couch. She had laid out her paints and the strange bottle of ink in a careful semicircle—small palettes filled with pigments, some cracked, some nearly gone. Her fingers were stained to the knuckles, and her shawl had slipped from one shoulder.

Andrew hesitated.

She looked up. Her eyes were dark, wide, and still. Not frightened. Not grateful. Just... watching.

"I brought you this," he said, setting the bowl on the low table beside her.

"Thank you," she said softly, her voice hoarse from fever and silence.

Andrew sat in the armchair, not too close. He watched her pick up the bowl and sip slowly. Her movements deliberate, almost ritualistic. She did not slurp or rush. She ate like someone who had learned to make every bite last.

He cleared his throat. "You paint a lot?"

She nodded.

"Where do the images come from?"

She took a few moments before she answered. Her gaze drifted to the canvas in front of her. The painting had changed since he had last seen it. The ship was still there, but now there was a figure at the helm—tall, cloaked, faceless. Behind it, the sky burned violet, and something winged moved in the distance.

"I don't know," she said finally. "They just come."

Andrew leaned forward slightly. "Do you dream them?"

"Sometimes," she whispered. "Sometimes I see them before I sleep. Sometimes after."

He studied her face. There was something too still about her. Not just sick—anchored. Like she was holding something inside that did not belong to her.

"You are not from here," he said after a moment.

She shook her head. "I came from the bayou. I followed the sound of bells."

Andrew frowned. "Streetcar bells?"

"No," she said. "Older ones."

He did not ask what she meant. He was not sure he wanted to know.

She set the bowl down and picked up a brush, dipping it into the bottle of ink that was now a deep green. Her hand moved with quiet precision, adding a line to the horizon of the painting—a crack in the sky.

Andrew watched her work, the silence stretching between them.

"You are not afraid of me," he said.

She paused. "Should I be?"

He did not answer.

She turned, her eyes meeting his. "You're not just one thing."

Andrew furrowed his brow in confusion.

"You're two," she said. "But they don't fight. They wait."

He stood abruptly; the chair creaking behind him. "I should go check on Korlue."

She nodded, already returning to her painting.

As he stepped into the hallway, he glanced back once. Nideya was adding the last stroke to the canvas—a small figure in the distance, walking toward the faceless one. It had short white hair.

Andrew moved down the hallway slowly, the floorboards creaking beneath his steps. The apartment felt different now—as if something had shifted in its bones. The air was still heavy, but charged, as if the walls themselves were listening.

He reached the kitchen doorway and paused.

Korlue was leaning against the counter, arms folded, staring out the window into the dark. The pot on the stove had been turned off, and the ladle rested in the sink. The light above him cast a soft glower across his face, highlighting the tension in his jaw, the quiet exhaustion in his eyes.

Andrew stepped inside. "She is... strange."

Korlue did not look at him. "She's scared."

"I do not believe that," Andrew said. "But there is something else. She said I am not just one thing. That I am two. And they do not fight—they wait."

Korlue turned then, slowly. "She said that?"

Andrew nodded. "She sees things. I do not think she is just gifted. I think she is something older. Something that does not know it is old. At least what is in her blood is."

Korlue's gaze was steady. "You think she's dangerous?"

Andrew hesitated. "No. But I think she is hiding what she is."

Korlue's brow furrowed. "Why?"

"I do not know," Andrew replied. "But I believe she may be an oracle. Possibly more."

Korlue pushed off the counter and crossed the room, stopping just in front of him. "You're shaken."

Andrew met his eyes. "I killed a child once, and I do not have the best track record with oracles. I killed the last two I came into contact with."

Korlue reached up, brushing a strand of hair from Andrew's temple. "I don't think you'll hurt her."

Andrew closed his eyes briefly, leaning into the touch. "I want to be better. For you and for her."

"Then stay. Don't vanish when it gets hard," he said, his voice quiet.

"I will not," Andrew said. "Not this time."

They stood there for a moment, the silence between them no longer sharp, but soft—like the hush before a storm.

From the sitting room, the sound of brush against canvas resumed. Slow and steady.

Andrew turned toward the hallway, then back to Korlue. "I am tired and in need of a shower."

Korlue nodded. "Then go shower. I'll join you after I clean up down here and put Nideya in the guest room."

Andrew nodded, then gave Korlue a chaste kiss on the lips before heading to their room.

As he stepped into the shower, the hot water washing over his tired skin, he smiled. He had made amends with Korlue, or at least he was working toward that, but his smile faded when he remembered Nideya's painting. The ship looked like the Pale Emperor, and the white-haired figure could have been Korlue. But who was the other figure? Why did the painting unsettle him so? He would get his answers in the morning when he was not so tired.

CHAPTER 20

The sun had not yet broken the horizon, but the heat was already rising—thick and damp, curling through the open windows like breath. The house was quiet; the city outside was still half asleep. Streetcars had not begun their clatter, and the only sound was the distant hum of cicadas and the creak of old floorboards.

Nideya crept down the hallway, her satchel slung over one shoulder, her canvas tucked under her arm. Her shoes were tied together and dangled from the strap—she had not wanted the sound of her soles on the wood to betray her. She moved like she had on the streets. Light, fast, invisible.

She did not want to leave, not really. The bed had been soft. The soup had been warm. Korlue spoke to her as if she mattered. But comfort was dangerous. She still did not know these people. It was nice of them to take her in when she collapsed, but they were not human. She did not fully trust them yet. Though she was still not feeling well, she needed to leave. It was better for them if she did.

"Nideya."

She froze.

Andrew's voice was low, but it carried. She turned slowly, canvas clutched tight against her chest.

He was standing at the end of the hallway, barefoot and shirtless. He had patches of black scales in random places on his torso that shimmered with a green tint in the morning light. His eyes, a jeweled green, were sharp, not angry—just awake in a way that made her feel seen.

"Where are you going so early?" he asked. "It is dangerous out there."

"I can take care of myself," she said, her voice steady despite the tremor in her chest.

Andrew raised a brow. "You are still feverish. You are in no condition to be out on your own."

"I'm fine," she said, clutching her satchel tighter. "I don't wanna be a burden."

"You will not be," he replied. "You are not safe out there."

She did not respond.

"There is a killer on the loose in the Quarter. He is feeding. Age and consent do not matter to him."

Nideya's grip tightened on the canvas. "I'll be all right."

"I believe you," he said, stepping closer, his voice softening. "But you do not have to be alone."

She looked up at him, searching for the catch. There was always a catch.

"I am not asking you to trust us," he said. "I am asking you to be smart and stay alive."

She hesitated. The hallway felt longer than it had a moment ago. The door heavier. Her satchel suddenly felt too light. She knew that asking her to stay was hard for him. She had heard their conversation before being sent out of the room. Yet he was trying.

"Why do you care?" she asked, wanting to know his reason for wanting her to stay.

This time, he hesitated. "Because Korlue does, and so do I. It would be wrong to let you leave when you have no place to go."

But she did have a safe place to go; she just could not find it on her own. She found she missed Celestine and Émile. They were like family to her.

"Nideya?" He had stepped closer without her noticing. What was he that he could move so fast, so quietly? "Are you well?"

She backed into the door. "I'm fine," she murmured. She was not fine, however. She was terrified of being with two men she did not know, who were monsters. And they were in danger. Then she remembered what her mother had written. She needed to be brave. "I'll stay," she said after a moment. "But I won't be a guest."

Andrew nodded. "You will work once you are well again. Help Korlue in the store. Clean, inventory, whatever he needs."

"I can do that."

"You will earn your keep," he continued. "But you will be safe with us."

She nodded.

He stepped back, giving her space. "But if you stay, you stay honest. No more sneaking out. No hiding."

She nodded again, slower this time.

He gestured back toward the stairs. "Go eat. I will tell Korlue you are staying."

She walked past him; her steps light but deliberate, the canvas still pressed to her chest. She would not tell him what she was. Not yet. Not until she knew whether her dreams were safe here.

She did not look back as she ascended the stairs toward the kitchen, but the canvas pressed against her ribs felt heavier with each step. Not because of its size, but because of what it showed. She had painted late that night. Her fingers had moved faster than her thoughts, guided by something older than memory. The brush had carved shadows into the ship's deck—wood slick with blood and salt. The surrounding sea was black, not from night, but from something deeper. Something wrong.

Andrew stood at the center of the painting, his shirt torn, his mouth open in a silent cry. It was the same as before, but this time he held a sword. She could not tell if it was raised in attack or defense. And opposite him loomed a figure—tall, faceless, cloaked in shadow still. No eyes, no mouth, just a suggestion of form again. The kind of thing that haunted dreams and lingered in the corners of waking thought.

The faceless figure held something in its hand. A shard of glass? A bone? Nideya had not decided. It did not matter. The object pulsed with the same color she had used for the inside of an ornate cup in one of her other paintings—deep crimson, like old blood.

She had not meant to paint Andrew again. She had tried to avoid him. But he kept appearing. In fragments. In echoes. Always on the edge of violence. Always on a ship.

She did not know if it was memory or prophecy. She only knew it felt true.

And truth was dangerous.

She reached the kitchen and set the canvas down, face-down on the table. She did not want them to see it. Not yet. Not until she understood what it meant. Because if Andrew was fighting that thing again—if he was still bound to it—then this house was not a shelter. It was a battleground.

And she had just agreed to stay.

CHAPTER 21

T he bell above the door chimed softly, barely audible over the rain tapping at the windows. Korlue looked up from the counter, fingers still resting on the spine of a half-shelved volume. The man who entered wore a long coat, collar turned high, and a wide-brimmed hat that cast his face in shadow. He moved like memory—familiar, unsettling.

"Back again," Korlue said, his voice cautious but curious.

Jonas did not answer immediately. He stepped deeper into the store, the scent of the sea and decay mingling around him. His gloved hand rested briefly on a bookcase, as if steadying himself.

"I need your help," he said finally, his voice low and frayed. "The book you sold me—it speaks of the Tidevault, but not clearly. I'm running out of time."

Korlue studied him. "You look worse than before."

Jonas gave a soft laugh, dry as parchment. "I *am* worse than before." He lingered near the poetry section, his posture careful, his face still hidden. "You've changed your hair," he said almost absently. "Shorter. It suits you."

Korlue blinked, caught off guard. "Thank you. I wasn't sure about it."

"It frames your face. Makes your eyes sharper." He paused. "Andrew didn't like it, did he?"

Korlue stiffened. "You know about Andrew?"

"I know more than I should," Jonas murmured. "I've had eyes on this place. On you."

At that, Korlue's breath hitched. "Why?"

Jonas stepped closer, still cloaked in shadow. "Because I remember the way you danced... and the way you ran."

Silence stretched between them, taut and trembling.

Korlue did not move. "You shouldn't be here."

"I had nowhere else to go," he replied.

"You should've gone to the authorities."

Jonas' head tilted slightly. "Why would I do that?"

"You're the one they've been whispering about," Korlue said, his voice steady.

A natural flash of lightning made Korlue flinch and revealed a grin on Jonas' face. "You know what I am?"

"I do," Korlue nodded. "An incubus. A killer."

Jonas flinched, just barely.

"I've seen the bodies," Korlue continued. "Drained. Empty. You fed on them."

He walked slowly along the row, lightly brushing his fingers across the spines. "I had to."

"No," Korlue said firmly. "You chose to."

Once again, silence bloomed between them, thick and bitter.

"I won't help you," Korlue said, determined not to fall under his spell again. "Not with the chalice. Not with anything. You need to turn yourself in."

Jonas moved closer, shadows clinging to him like regret. "They'll burn me."

"They should."

Jonas' gloved hand trembled as he reached for the collar of his coat. Slowly, he unbuttoned it, revealing the pale curve of a scar along his throat—jagged, ancient, still faintly bruised and tinted green. "I didn't always feed like this," he started. "I was stronger once. Controlled. But this changed that."

Korlue's breath caught. "How did you get that?"

"A dragon. A beautiful, terrible thing. I provoked him. Hurt someone he loved. I wanted to see if he'd break."

"And did he?" Korlue whispered.

"He bit me," Jonas said. "His venom was fast, but I'm also a water elemental, and he foolishly threw me to the sea. I got most of it out, but the infection still lingers," he explained. "Like I said, it's killing me slow, and I've held it off for over two centuries."

Korlue narrowed his eyes. "That's a long time."

"I have a strong will," Jonas grinned. "I want to live."

"Did Andrew do that to you?" he asked suspiciously.

"No," Jonas said after a moment. "My dragon was cruel and ruthless. Just the way I made him, but he's gone now."

"So you deserved what happened," he said flatly.

Jonas grinned again. "I suppose I did." He regarded Korlue curiously. "I'm not asking for forgiveness. Just a chance. If I find the chalice, I can stop feeding like this. I can stop killing."

Korlue shook his head. "You don't deserve redemption."

"And Andrew does?"

Outside, thunder rolled low across the sky. The rain thickened into a curtain, blurring the street lamps and washing the city in silver. Jonas stood on the threshold of the bookstore, coat collar raised, and his hat low over his eyes. He lingered for a breath—just long enough to look back at Korlue, who had not moved from behind the counter.

"You should leave now," he said in a low growl. He would not play Jonas' game.

Jonas tipped his hat. "If that is your wish." Then he stepped into the rain and vanished.

A moment later, Nideya came out from behind a bookcase where she had been hiding, watching. "That man is evil," she said, her voice low. "Gives me the shivers."

Korlue looked at her and the small stack of books she had pressed to her chest. "He's gone now, so don't worry about him."

"What if he comes back?" She set the books down on the counter.

"He won't if he knows what's good for him."

They both turned when the bell above the door chimed again. Andrew entered like a gust of wind, his coat soaked. He looked up and saw the two of them staring at him. Then he inhaled sharply, nostrils flaring, and his expression darkened.

"He was here," he said, his voice low and dangerous.

"You just missed him, actually," Korlue replied.

Andrew did not respond. He turned on his heel, already heading back into the storm, boots striking the floor like war drums.

Korlue watched him go, heart pounding, the scent of old paper and fading incense clinging to the air. Outside, thunder rolled again.

Twenty minutes had passed before the bell above the door rang again. Andrew burst in, soaked to the bone, his coat plastered to his broad frame, boots leaving muddy prints across the floor. His eyes scanned the shop like a predator scenting blood, jaw clenched, breath ragged.

"I could not track his scent in the rain," he said, low and furious. "He is gone. I lost him in the Quarter."

Korlue walked out from behind the counter. "That's not surprising. The storm's getting worse."

Andrew took off his coat and turned to him, eyes narrowing. "Did he touch you?"

"No."

"Did he feed?"

"How would I know?" he asked, his tone firm. "He came here to ask for help. He wanted me to help him find the Tidevault."

Andrew's expression darkened. "Of course he did."

Outside, the storm howled louder, the wind rattling the windows like a warning.

Andrew stepped closer, lowering his voice. "He is dangerous, Kory."

Korlue swallowed hard. "He's dying. But I told him to turn himself in."

Andrew froze.

"I tried anyway, but he refused," he continued.

"He will not turn himself in willingly. We will have to catch him."

Korlue sighed. "That won't be easy. Any luck finding his ship?"

Andrew shook his head, lightly spraying Korlue with rainwater from his hair. "He is smart and not keeping it docked here."

"Well, until we can find him, you should go get out of those wet clothes and warm up."

Andrew looked down at himself. He was dripping everywhere. "I am not cold, but I need to change. Perhaps we should close up early; the storm is relentless."

Korlue looked out of the window to see sheets of rain coming down and furiously pelting the street. "That's probably a good idea. No one will be out in this." He looked over at Nideya, who was watching the rain pour with wide eyes. She looked a little scared, and he wondered what she was thinking. "Nideya, honey. Are you all right?"

She blinked wildly for a moment, then nodded, going back to her shelving.

"Did you need help with closing?" Andrew asked softly.

"No," he said. "Nideya and I can handle things down here. You go change, and we'll be up when we're done."

Andrew nodded, giving Korlue a light kiss, before leaving to change.

Korlue went to Nideya and lightly tapped her shoulder, making her jump and squeak. "I didn't mean to scare you," he chuckled. "Are you sure you're all right?"

Again, she nodded, but Korlue did not believe her.

"It's okay if you're not," he said gently.

"I'm all right, really. I'm just worried about some friends in the bayou, that's all," she admitted.

"Oh," he said in surprise. "Why aren't you staying with them?"

She shrugged. "I outgrew the place, they said. I needed to find my own way."

Korlue was taken aback by her words but accepted them. He stopped her from shelving to help him close up the store. As they locked up and turned out the lights, Korlue thought about the things Jonas had said. He was not seeking forgiveness, but a chance. He wondered what he would do if he found the chalice and it healed him. Would he come back for him? To take him away from Andrew? His mate? His love?

The storm raged, and Jonas searched, while Korlue stood alarmed, the scent of rain and old paper thick around him.

CHAPTER 22

T he following day, the air was filled with the humidity that only summer storms could bring. Outside, a streetcar rattled down the street, its bell clanging like a distant heartbeat. A brass band played somewhere in the distance, its melody weaving through the humid air like a spell. Inside the bookstore was quiet, save for the soft rustle of pages and the occasional creak of the floorboards.

Korlue stood behind the counter, sorting a shipment of new volumes and rare editions. His shirt sleeves were rolled up, revealing ink-stained wrists. Nideya sat cross-legged in the corner, her nose buried in a book about fairies that had caught her attention, the waves of her hair catching the light like spun molasses.

Then the bell above the door jingled sharp and shrill, like a warning.

Madame Delphine entered like a storm dressed in silk. Her layered skirts swept the floor, and her turban—deep violet, embroidered with gold thread—sat like a crown atop her wild silver hair. She smelled of myrrh, river moss, and something older—something that did not belong to this century.

"Ah, there she is," she crooned, eyes locking on Korlue. "My little bolt of lightning. You've cut your hair! Why do you insist on hiding your femininity?"

Korlue did not look up. "I'm not a woman, Madame. We've talked about this."

She waved a hand, dismissing the correction like a fly. "The spirits don't care about your declarations. They see what's true. And you can't fool them with trousers and short hair."

He sighed, gently placing a book on the counter. "What can I help you with?"

She moved closer, eyes scanning the store like a priest inspecting a chapel. "I had another vision," she said, lowering her voice. "The spirits whispered last night."

Korlue rolled his eyes. She always spoke of spirits as if they were good friends.

"A man is coming," she continued. "Handsome. Dangerous. He will take you away from all of this. And soon."

Korlue met her gaze. "Madame, no one is coming to take me away."

Her eyes narrowed, then shifted to Nideya. Her expression soured instantly. "And who is that child?" she asked, her voice sharp.

"That's Nideya," he said, his tone one of warning. "She's staying with us."

Delphine sniffed. "Mixed blood. Trouble follows that kind. You don't know what she carries."

Nideya looked up, startled. Her eyes flicked to Korlue, uncertain.

Korlue's voice was low but firm. "She carries books and kindness. That's enough."

Delphine's lip curled. "You've lost your way," she fussed. "You used to listen to me. To the spirits."

"I still listen," he said. "But I don't let hate speak for them."

The silence that followed was heavy, like the air before a summer storm. Outside, a trumpet wailed from a nearby balcony, the notes bending with sorrow.

Delphine's eyes gleamed. "And that man you keep—he's a brute. I've seen it. His aura is red and cracked. Violence clings to him like sweat."

Korlue's jaw tightened. "Andrew is gentle. Protective. You don't know him."

"I know what the spirits show me," she snapped. "He will break you. Or worse—he will keep you from your path. From your family."

"That is enough, Madame," Korlue growled. "Andrew is my family, and so is Nideya."

Nideya looked wide-eyed but said nothing.

"You can't be here anymore if you can't accept them as such," he said firmly.

"You would cast me out?" she asked, her voice trembling—not with fear, but with fury.

"I would," he replied. He had had enough of her antics. "This store is a sanctuary. Not a stage for your bitterness."

Delphine stared at him, her eyes ancient and wounded. Then she turned, her heel striking the floor with finality. "He will come," she hissed. "And you will follow."

She swept out; the door slamming behind her. The windows rattle in their frames. Korlue exhaled slowly, the tension draining from his shoulders. He stared at Nideya, who was watching with wide, solemn eyes.

"You okay?" he asked.

She nodded. "She's scary. But you were brave."

He smiled, softer now. "Sometimes you have to choose truth over prophecy."

"You really think I'm family?" she wondered, a tear rolling down her cheek, but she wiped it away too quickly.

"Hm? Oh, yes. Of course!" He smiled. "Us misfits gotta stick together," he said with a wink.

Outside, twilight bruised the sky. But inside the bookstore, the air felt clearer—like something had been exorcised.

The door creaked open, and Andrew stepped in, his bare feet quiet against the floorboards. He smelled faintly of cypress and rain—like the bayou after a thunderstorm. His shirt was damp at the collar, his hair tousled from the wind. Korlue looked up from his book of folktales. His eyes softened at the sight of Andrew, but his shoulders did not quite relax. He carried a canvas satchel slung across his chest, a bouquet of wild irises peeking out—half-crushed, but still fragrant.

Andrew's eyes settled on Korlue. "Are you all right?" he asked, his voice low.

Korlue nodded, but the motion was slow, uncertain. "Delphine came by."

Andrew's jaw flexed. "What did she say this time?"

Korlue hesitated, then closed his book and got out of bed. "She said things. About me. About you."

Andrew's brow furrowed as he removed the satchel, but he did not interrupt.

"She called me her little bolt of lightning. Said violence clings to you like sweat." His voice was flat. "She said you'd keep me from my path. From my family."

Andrew crossed the room slowly. "Do you believe her?" he asked, quiet but firm.

Korlue met him halfway, shaking his head. "No, you're my family. I believe she sees something, though." His voice was steady, but there was a tremor beneath it. "She said a man is coming. Someone dangerous. Someone I'll follow."

"She has never cared for me. Perhaps she just wants me out of your life." He reached for Korlue's hands, grounding him.

"She doesn't hate you because of who you are," Korlue started. "She hates you because you're not the one she saw. You don't fit in her story."

Andrew stepped closer. "I do not want to be part of her story. I want to be part of yours."

Korlue looked at his hands—his slender fingers, Andrew's calloused ones. "She said I've lost my way."

Andrew gently brushed his hands. "You have lost nothing. You have chosen. That is the difference."

He looked at Andrew, his eyes searching. "What if the man she saw does come? What if it's Jonas?"

Andrew's voice did not waver. "I will not let him near you again. He will not hurt you," he said, as his grip tightened.

"I'm scared, Andy," he murmured, leaning into him, his forehead resting against Andrew's chest.

Andrew kissed the top of his head. "And I am here."

They stood there in each other's embrace for a long moment before Andrew spoke again.

"I could use a shower," he said in a low voice.

"Yes, you could," Korlue agreed, stepping back.

"Care to join me?" he asked suggestively, his eyes glassy and hooded with lust.

Korlue grinned. "Only if you promise to behave."

"I will make no such promises," he growled, picking Korlue up.

With a small flex of his power, their clothes burned away.

"Andrew!" he gasped.

"What? It will save us time," he grinned, carrying him into the bathroom.

They kissed as the hot water rushed over their bodies, their tongues touching and playing. Andrew had Korlue against the shower wall, his long, thin legs wrapped around his waist.

"I thought you wanted to get clean," Korlue said between pants.

"I wish to make you dirty first," Andrew replied.

Korlue whimpered as the head of Andrew's cock found his sensitive ring. He pushed past the tight, stubborn muscles with considerable effort.

"I need you to relax," Andrew murmured into the side of his throat.

Andrew kissed along Korlue's jaw and neck, stopping to suckle at his pulse point. Korlue tensed up when he felt the tip of his lover's fangs, but they did not pierce his flesh. He relaxed when he felt Andrew chuckle.

"I have no need of your blood tonight," he purred. "Just your body."

With one stroke, Andrew filled Korlue's tight ass. He was slow and gentle with each thrust after, taking his time to show how much he cared. Korlue panted and clung to Andrew's strong body as if it were a lifeline. Andrew grunted as he pumped into him, picking up his pace. Korlue raked his nails across the open, non-scaled parts of Andrew's back, arching his own as he felt his release. Blood trickled down Andrew's back as he continued to pump in and out of him.

The scent of Andrew's blood made Korlue's senses go crazy, and he bared his fangs, sinking them into the space between Andrew's neck and shoulder. Andrew stopped mid-thrust at the sensation, his breath catching. It took him a moment to regain his wits and continue his thrusts. He finished in several more long, glorious strokes, filling Korlue with his seed.

They stayed there for a long moment, breathing heavily.

"Thank you," Andrew whispered, kissing Korlue's throat.

"For what?" Korlue asked curiously.

And set Korlue back down and looked him in the eyes. "For being with me all this time. For choosing me."

Korlue cupped his face. "I love you. All of you."

"I love you, too," he smiled.

"Now, let's get cleaned up and out of here. I'm tired."

"As am I," Andrew agreed.

They got cleaned up, with Andrew giving Korlue one last orgasm because he could not help himself, and got ready for bed. They unbraided and brushed each other's hair, though tired as they were. Not bothering to get dressed, they turned out the lights and climbed into bed. Andrew was the first to pass out, but Korlue's mind was suddenly alert.

Despite Andrew's reassurances, Korlue had a fitful night. He could not help but think about Madam Delphin's predictions, as absurd as they were, as he tossed and turned in an attempt to get comfortable. Would he really follow Jonas and leave Andrew behind? He knew he would never leave Andrew willingly. But he could not help worrying as he dreamed of the incubus that haunted him.

CHAPTER 23

T he scent of old paper and chicory coffee hung thick in the air, mingling with the sweet trace of powdered sugar as Nideya balanced a stack of worn hardcovers against her hip. Morning light slanted through the tall windows of Bound to Please, catching motes of dust in its golden net. She moved slowly, deliberately, her fingers trailing the spines of books as if they might whisper secrets if touched just right.

Korlue was somewhere behind the counter, humming low and tuneless as he sorted receipts. Nideya liked the quiet rhythm of the shop, the way it felt suspended in time—like stepping into a dream stitched together by ink and longing.

The bell above the door jingled, and she did not need to turn to know it was Lucian. He always came around this time, bearing a plate of beignets wrapped in wax paper and a grin too wide for his face.

"Delivery for da book wizard," he announced, setting the plate down with a flourish. "And his mysterious assistant."

Nideya glanced over her shoulder, arching a brow. "I'm not an assistant."

Lucian shrugged, undeterred. "Muse, den. Or enchantress. Ya paint weird t'in's. Dat counts."

She snorted softly and turned back to the shelf, sliding a copy of The Picture of Dorian Gray into place. "You think everything's magic."

"Ya say dat like it's a bad t'in'," he replied, falling into step behind her as she moved to the next aisle. "Dis place is magic. I told you dat da first day I met ya."

She remembered. He had said it with such conviction, standing in the doorway with powdered sugar on his chin and eyes wide as saucers. She had not known what to make of him then—still did not, really—but there was something about his presence that softened the edges of her usual wariness.

Lucian leaned close to peer at the titles she was sorting. "Why does Mista Young hate dis one?" He tapped a slim volume with a cracked spine.

"He doesn't hate it," Nideya said, amused. "He just thinks Korlue's taste is too sentimental."

Lucian grinned. "Mista Young's fussy. Like a cat dat only drinks rainwater."

Nideya laughed, a real laugh, the kind that startled her with its brightness. "That's… actually perfect."

They moved together through the rows, shelving books and trading stories. Lucian asked about her paintings—why they always had three stars in them, why the eyes never looked quite human. She deflected with half-truths and riddles, and he did not seem to mind. He liked the mystery.

At one point, he tried to balance a stack of poetry books on his head and nearly toppled into a display of antique maps. Nideya caught his arm just in time, and they both dissolved into laughter, breathless and tangled in the moment.

For a little while, the world outside faded—the jazz drifting in from the street, the heat pressing against the windows, the ache that sometimes curled in her chest when she thought too hard about the past. In Bound to Please, surrounded by stories and strange boys with sugar-dusted fingers, Nideya felt almost like she belonged.

Korlue heard the laughter before he saw them—light, unguarded, echoing through the aisles like a breeze stirring old pages. He paused, one hand resting on the edge of the counter, the other still dusted with powdered sugar from Lucian's beignets. Nideya's laugh was rare, a sound he had come to treasure like a secret passage in a well-worn book. And Lucian—well, Lucian had a way of coaxing joy from shadows.

He leaned slightly, catching sight of them between the shelves. Nideya was shelving books with her usual grace, but her shoulders were looser today, her movements less careful. Lucian trailed behind her, animated and clumsy, gesturing wildly as he described some ridiculous theory about Andrew's reading habits. She was smiling—really smiling—and Korlue felt something shift inside him.

Not jealousy. Not loss.

Relief.

She was opening up.

For several days, she had moved through the shop like a ghost stitched into flesh—present, but distant. Her paintings spoke in riddles, her silences louder than any confession. He had worried, quietly, the way he always did. Worried that Bound to Please might not be enough to hold her. That he might not be enough.

But now, watching her laugh with Lucian, he felt something else: hope.

Lucian was harmless, yes, but more than that—he was kind. Curious. He saw magic in everything, even in Nideya's strange stars and haunted eyes. And she let him see her. Not all of her, not yet. But enough.

Korlue turned back to the counter, brushing sugar from his fingers. He picked up the ledger again, though the numbers meant little now. The shop was quiet, but alive. The kind of quiet that held stories in its bones.

He did not interrupt. Did not call out or ask for help with inventory. He simply listened, letting their laughter fill the space like music.

And for the first time in days, he smiled without hesitation.

CHAPTER 24

T he vision had come like a flood—colors surging through her fingers, breath stolen by something ancient and furious. Nideya did not remember standing, did not remember reaching for the brush. Only the feeling: a man rising from the deep, eyes like glaciers, mouth full of salt and vengeance.

Now she lay curled on the floor of her room in the apartment above the bookstore, her small body limp beside the canvas. The painting stared back at her—a man, tall, elegant, terrible. He was cloaked in seafoam and shadow, reaching through the waves toward Korlue.

She sat up slowly, her limbs trembling, and turned toward the easel. The painting stood there like a wound—fresh, glistening, alive. She had painted it in a trance; the vision pouring out of her like blood. She knew him. The incubus. The one who whispered death into the city's breath.

Korlue was beside her now, crouched low, his hand warm on her shoulder. His face was pale, his eyes locked on the painting.

"That's Jonas," he gasped.

Nideya blinked. "You know him?"

"Yes, I met him weeks ago. He was... magnetic. Too perfect. People were dying. I didn't connect him to it until Andrew said what he was." His voice was light, haunted. "He was here the other day. Why did you paint him?"

Before she could answer, the door creaked open and Andrew stepped in. His boots thudded against the floor, his suspenders hanging loose over his shirt. He looked tired, irritable—but when his eyes landed on the painting, something shifted. He stopped mid-step, staring. His face drained of color.

"No," he said, his voice low and brittle. "It cannot be him."

Nideya looked up, startled. "You know him, too?"

Andrew's jaw clenched. "He tortured me. A very long time ago. I bit him—pumped him full of my venom, then threw him to the sea. He is dead."

"Wait, you are the dragon that bit him?" Korlue stood slowly, his voice calm but firm. "Andrew, I know this man. He's the incubus in the city, and he's alive. He's been in the shop."

Nideya watched Andrew closely. He did not respond right away. He stepped closer to the painting, his eyes narrowing. His breath hitched, and for a moment, the flaring anger had faded, replaced by something else—uncertainty. Memory.

"I killed him," Andrew whispered. "Alexander Tempest is dead."

"But I saw him," Korlue spoke.

Andrew's hand trembled as he reached toward the canvas, stopping just short of touching it. His eyes flicked to Korlue, then to Nideya. "It cannot be," he said. "It is not possible. He should be dead."

"But he's not," Korlue said. "And if Nideya saw him in a vision—"

Andrew's face twisted. "Visions. She is a child, Korlue. Sick. Delirious."

"She's telling the truth," Korlue argued.

Andrew turned on her, his voice rising. "You think painting nightmares makes them real? You think you can scare us into believing your fever dreams?"

"I didn't mean to—" she began, but her voice faltered. He was not listening.

"You are a child," he said coldly. "Korlue took you in out of pity, and now you are twisting it. You are trying to manipulate us."

"Andrew, stop this! You're scaring her," Korlue shouted. "She's telling the truth! That is the incubus you hunt." He pointed to the painting.

"He is not," Andrew snapped. "You are being fooled. And you—" he turned back to Nideya, eyes blazing, "you are feeding into it. That man is dead! You are working with a shapeshifter. One who is trying to con us out of something. What game are the two of you playing at?"

The words hit like a slap. Nideya's breath caught, her chest tightening. She scrambled to her feet, clutching the quilt around her shoulders, and bolted past them. Down the narrow staircase, past the rows of books that smelled like safety and stories, through the back door and into the alley behind the store.

The damp August heat wrapped around her like a second fever. She pressed her back against the brick wall and slid down, knees to chest, tears streaking her cheeks. She had thought she was safe here. That she had finally found a home. But she was wrong.

Above her, the attic room glowed with morning light. Somewhere inside, the painting waited—silent, damning, true. She had done her part, warned them. Now she could return to the bayou where she belonged. With Celestine and Émile.

CHAPTER 25

T he wind clawed at the windows of the apartment above the bookstore, rattling the glass like a warning. Korlue stood in the guest room, shoulders tense, lightning humming faintly beneath his skin. The storm was coming fast—he could feel it in the pressure behind his eyes, in the static crawling along his spine. It did not seem natural.

"You had no right to speak to her like that," he snapped, his voice sharp as broken glass. "She's a child, Andrew. She has no control over her powers, and she's scared. And you—"

Andrew stood frozen, his eyes locked on the painting. "I killed him," he repeated. "I *know* I did."

Korlue stood beside the painting, arms crossed, gaze steady. "Then how do you explain this? How do you explain how I know him? Have seen him? Touched him? Talked to him?"

Andrew's jaw clenched. "I cannot. Maybe it is a trick. Many oracles can see into the past as well as the future."

"But he's been here," Korlue spat.

Andrew turned away, pacing the length of the small room. The floorboards creaked beneath his boots. He ran a hand over his tightly braided hair, his fingers trembling. "He kept me chained in a cave," he said suddenly. "I was young, eighteen at the time. He said he liked the way dragons screamed."

Korlue's breath caught, his anger fading, but he did not interrupt.

"He fed off pain. Not just mine. Others. He would bring them in, one by one. He made me watch." Andrew's voice cracked. "I died down there. Many times. He pulled all my scales off and made jewelry from them."

He stopped pacing, staring out the window at the rooftops of the Quarter. Korlue felt sick hearing the pain in his lover's voice at recalling such painful memories. He did not know what he had been through, and at the hands of Jonas.

"When I bit him, I did not hold back," he continued. "I gave him everything. Enough venom to kill a leviathan. He convulsed. I dragged him across the beach and threw him into the sea. I watched him sink."

Korlue stepped closer. "But he didn't die."

Andrew turned, eyes blazing. "What does that mean? That he is back to finish what he started?"

Korlue saw the panic behind the rage. He looked at the painting again. "It means Nideya's vision wasn't just a dream. It was a warning."

Andrew's shoulders sagged. He looked older suddenly, worn thin by memories. "I cannot go back to that life, Kory. I will not go back."

"I don't think he's here for you," Korlue said quietly. "I think he wants me."

Andrew's rage flared again, warming the room. "He cannot have you!" he growled. "You belong to me!"

Korlue's eyes narrowed. "I'm not a thing to possess," he said through gritted teeth. "And Nideya is out there all alone."

Andrew paced again, his jaw tight, eyes flashing between guilt and defiance. "She is dangerous."

"She's alone," Korlue argued. "And if you had even a shred of decency left, you'd go find her before the storm hits."

Lightning cracked inside, illuminating Andrew's face in stark relief, and leaving a scorch mark on the floor where it had hit. He hesitated, then cursed under his breath before leaving the room.

Korlue watched him disappear down the stairs, the door slamming behind him like a final warning.

The silence that followed was deafening. Korlue exhaled slowly, the tension in his chest refusing to ease. He moved toward the stairs, descending into the bookstore below, where the scent of old paper and incense mingled with the damp air. It was grounding in its comfort. He would not bother opening that day; the storm was coming too fast, but he felt safe in the store.

The shop was dim, lit only by the flickering gas lamps and the occasional flash of lightning through the front windows. Shelves loomed like sentinels, rows of forgotten stories and half-truths. He moved behind the counter, trying to steady his breath. The storm was pressing in, thick and electric. The storm would catch Andrew and Nideya. They would have to find shelter elsewhere until it passed if they did not get back soon.

Then the bell above the door gave a soft, deliberate chime. Korlue turned toward the door. It had been locked.

A hooded figure stood in the doorway, rain dripping from his coat, the lock rusted at his feet. The air around him was unnaturally still. The storm seemed to pause, as if holding its breath.

"How did you... you should stay inside," he said, his voice calm but wary. "It's not safe out there."

The figure stepped forward, water pooling around his boots. He pulled back his hood. "I'm not here for shelter," he spoke, his voice a velvet rasp.

Korlue's stomach dropped. The man's eyes gleamed like ice, and his presence felt like drowning. "Jonas," Korlue breathed. The name tasted like rust on his tongue.

The storm outside seemed to surge in response, a gust slamming against the windows. Korlue reached instinctively for the grounding necklace at his throat, his fingers brushing the smooth obsidian.

He must have fed well again, because Jonas moved first. Korlue did not have time to think. He ran. Jonas moved like a wave—fluid, fast, merciless.

They collided in the narrow aisle between poetry and occult history. Korlue struck with precision, lightning sparking from his fingertips, but he held back. The store was sacred. Though he was angry with him, it was his and Andrew's home.

Jonas fought like water and hunger—his blows serpentine, his touch cold and invasive. Korlue felt the pull in his veins, the unnatural tug of blood trying to obey someone else's will. He gritted his teeth and surged back, slamming Jonas into a shelf of alchemic texts.

Then...

"Kory?" came an innocent voice. "Mama told me to bring you some beignets."

Lucian's voice rang out, bright and familiar. The boy had braved the storm, a plate of beignets in his hands, powdered sugar dusting his fingers.

Korlue's heart seized. "Lucian, get out!"

But Jonas turned, eyes narrowing.

"No!" Korlue lunged, lightning crackling from his palms—but Jonas was faster.

With a flick of his wrist. A twist of blood.

Lucian collapsed, the packed plate shattering beside him, sugar blooming across the floor like snow over a grave.

Korlue screamed. The sound tore from his throat, raw and electric. He surged forward, fury eclipsing restraint, lightning arcing wildly—but Jonas caught him mid-strike, fingers digging into Korlue's chest.

Pain bloomed. His blood turned against him.

He felt a final blow to the temple. The world spun.

As darkness claimed him, Korlue saw it. His grounding necklace, torn from his neck, lay among the broken porcelain and scattered beignets. An ornate black thing taking its place around his throat.

Then—nothing.

CHAPTER 26

The rain had turned the streets into rivers, and the wind howled through the alleys like a chorus of ghosts. Andrew moved fast, his boots splashing through puddles, his heart pounding with guilt and urgency. He did not know where she had gone—only that she had run, and that he had driven her to it.

He needed to find her fast. After finding out that Tempest—or Jonas, or whatever name the devil wore now—was still alive, he did not want to leave Korlue alone for longer than he had to.

The face in the painting that stared back at him—unchanged by time, untouched by death—had a scar beneath his jaw that ran down the side of his neck. It was faint, but unmistakable.

Andrew had carved it himself, with his own fangs, in a moment of desperate defiance. He remembered the taste of blood, the surge of venom, the sound of waves as he dragged the man's body to the edge of the beach and hurled him into the sea. For over two centuries, he was free of the demon. Now he was back and wanted his mate.

He shook the thought and memories out of his head. He needed to focus. To find Nideya. To get back to Korlue.

He found her in the shell of an old building near the edge of the Quarter, its windows shattered, its bones sagging with age and neglect. She was curled in the corner, her knees drawn to her chest, and soaked through and shivering.

"Nideya," he said, breathless.

She looked up, eyes blazing. "Don't you dare say my name like you care."

Andrew flinched. The fury in her voice was sharp, but beneath it he heard the tremble. "I did not mean—what I said back there. I was wrong."

"You called me sick and delirious. Said I was tryin' to con you."

"I was frightened," he admitted. "And foolish. I am sorry."

She did not answer. The wind shrieked through the broken windows, and lightning lit the room in stark flashes. Andrew stepped closer, careful not to crowd her.

"May I sit?" he asked.

She shrugged.

They sat in silence for a while; the storm raging outside. The building creaked and groaned, but it held.

Andrew glanced at her, the way her fingers traced invisible lines on the floor, like she was drawing something only she could see. He sighed. He was not good with children.

"What is it like?" he asked softly. "Your powers."

Nideya hesitated. Her voice when it came was quiet. "They're tied to my art. I don't just draw—I feel things.

Memories, emotions. Sometimes they come from me. Sometimes they come from other people. I sketch them, and they... become real."

Andrew blinked. "Real how?"

She looked at him, eyes dark and ancient. "Sometimes they move. Sometimes they speak. And sometimes they bleed."

He swallowed. "That is... unusual."

"It's dangerous," she said. "I don't always control it. That's why I stay quiet. That's why I don't let people close."

Andrew nodded, the weight of her words settling in his chest. "I did not realize. I should have asked. Should have listened."

"You're different, too," she murmured. "You and Korlue."

It was his turn to hesitate. "Yes, we are very different. He is a lightning elemental dhampir."

She narrowed her eyes at him. "And you?"

"Me? I am an Andr—a dragon of sorts," he said, opening his hand with the palm up and producing a small green flame.

He watched her for any kind of reaction, but there was none. She just went back to her drawing.

Outside, thunder cracked like a gunshot. Andrew flinched, and the flame went out. He instinctively glanced toward the door.

"You wanna go back," she said, still drawing.

"I need to," he admitted. "Korlue... something felt wrong when I left."

She did not argue. Instead, she pulled her blanket tighter and leaned against the wall, eyes distant. "We'll wait," she said. "The storm's not done with us yet."

Andrew watched her fingers twitch as the storm raged on, tracing invisible patterns on the warped floorboards. Her eyes were vacant, but her hands moved with a quiet urgency, like something inside her refused to be still.

"You said your art makes things real," he murmured. "But how?"

She paused for a moment. Then, slowly, she rolled up her sleeve.

Beneath her skin, faint veins shimmered—not blue, not red, but a deep, iridescent violet, like ink suspended in moonlight. It pulsed faintly, as if aware of being seen.

"It's not just my power," she said. "It's the ink. It's in me."

Andrew leaned closer, amazed and cautious.

"Ms. Celestine said it was made from a fallen star," she whispered. "And fairy blood. It doesn't dry out. It doesn't fade. And it never runs out."

He stared, transfixed. "It is alive."

She nodded. "It compels me. When I don't paint, it wriggles. It dreams. Shows me things I don't wanna see."

Lightning split the sky, casting her face in vivid contrast. For a moment, Andrew saw something ancient behind her eyes—something that had watched centuries pass through a veil of ink and longing.

"Does it hurt?" he asked.

"Only when I don't listen."

Suddenly, her eyes rolled back, showing only white. Her fingers moved quickly, almost feverishly, and the ink bled from her skin onto the floorboards, forming shapes that shimmered and shifted. A storm cloud. A ship. And a face—Korlue's—half formed and flickering.

Andrew's breath caught. "You painted him again."

"I didn't mean to," she said, panicked. "The ink paints what it wants. Or maybe... what I fear."

Outside, the storm began to soften, but inside the ruined building, something deeper had been unleashed. Not just a confession—but a connection. And the ink, restless and eternal, whispered between them.

CHAPTER 27

The ship rocked gently beneath him. Its hull groaned with age and secrets. Korlue sat on the edge of a cot, shirt torn and chest bandaged, the pain still blooming beneath his ribs where Jonas had carved through him. The necklace around his throat—sleek, black, deceptively elegant—throbbed faintly against his skin. A power dampener. He could feel it like a muzzle on his soul.

Jonas had clasped it on him after their fight, with a lover's touch and a captor's precision.

The door creaked open.

Jonas entered, his coat dripping seawater, his eyes gleaming with something too smooth to be human. He moved like tidewater—slow, purposeful, impossible to predict.

"I brought you something," he said.

Two crewmen dragged in a woman—pale and trembling, her mouth gagged with a cloth—her wrists bound by rope. Her eyes met Korlue's, wide and pleading.

"She's clean," Jonas said. "No disease. No enchantments. Just warm blood. You'll need it to heal."

Korlue's jaw tightened. "I won't feed."

Jonas' smile was soft. "She's going to die. Either by your hands or mine. And I won't be gentle."

Korlue looked at the woman. She was young. Human. Terrified.

"No," Korlue spat. "I won't do it."

Jonas grinned. "All right, then. You can watch her die, and I'll bring in another for you."

"Why are you doing this?" Korlue demanded. He did not understand the need for violence.

With a light touch to the woman's exposed arm, Jonas closed his eyes, a wide smile on his pale face. The woman screamed as best she could as her arm began to shrivel, as if it were losing all moisture.

"Stop it!" Korlue cried. "You're hurting her!"

"I told you, I won't be gentle. Now, feed and heal yourself, or I finish what I started."

Jonas pushed her into his arms. Korlue could feel her pulse, the warmth of her life flickering like a candle. He hated himself for what he was about to do.

"I'll make it peaceful," he whispered.

She nodded, tears slipping down her cheeks.

His fangs slipped easily into her skin. He fed. Just enough. Just until her breathing slowed, her body sagged, and her soul slipped free without pain. He held her hand until the end. Afterward, he fought tears that threatened to come. He had taken a life for the first time, and it did not sit well with him.

Jonas watched in silence, then had the crewmen remove the body.

"You're beautiful when you surrender," he said.

Korlue did not answer. He turned away, wiping his mouth, the taste of guilt thick on his tongue.

Jonas stepped closer. "You could be more than this. You could be mine."

Korlue flinched as Jonas' fingers brushed his jaw—cool and damp, like river mist. The incubus within Jonas was rising now, subtle and insidious. The air thickened. Korlue's breath caught.

"I remember the way you looked at me," Jonas murmured. "Before the fight. Before you know what I was. You wanted me."

"I wanted to kill you," Korlue hissed.

Jonas' laugh was soft. "Same thing, sometimes." He leaned in, lips nearly brushing Korlue's ear. "I could give you pleasure so deep it drowns you. I could make you forget the pain. The boy. The guilt."

Korlue's hand shot up, gripping Jonas's wrist. "I want to go back."

Jonas stilled. "Back?"

"To Andrew," Korlue spat. "He's my home."

Jonas' face twisted into something vile and hideous. The seduction curled into rage.

"You love him," he said in a low voice.

Korlue did not answer.

Jonas' eyes darkened. "You think he'll still want you? After what I'm going to do to you?"

Korlue's voice was steady. "He already does. He'll come for me."

Jonas threw Korlue against the wall, knocking the wind out of him. He pinned him there, breath hot, body pressing close. His erection, long and dangerous, rubbed against Korlue. The scent of the sea and decay was stronger this close. The dampener flared, choking Korlue's power. He braced for pain, for violation—but Jonas stopped, and his hand trembled.

"You're lucky I still want you alive," he said, his eyes locked with Korlue's.

Korlue spat blood. "You're afraid."

Jonas stepped back, his eyes burning. "Of your dragon? No," he grinned. "I broke him once, I'll do it again."

Korlue froze.

"But he would have to find us first."

"Nideya will help him," Korlue blurted out, covering his mouth in an attempt to pull the words back in.

Jonas raised a curious brow. "The little painter girl? What does she have to do with anything?"

Korlue said nothing.

"Ah, that's right, she's an oracle," he mused. "She painted my future. Didn't she?"

Korlue stared, his eyes burning with rage, but still said nothing.

Jonas smiled broadly. "Then it'll be a race to find the Tidevault." He turned on his heel and left.

Later, two more crewmen came. They chained Korlue in the brig, deep in the ship's belly, where the walls wept salt and the air tasted of rust. The necklace pulsed against his throat, a constant reminder of his powerlessness.

Jonas' voice echoed down the stairwell. "If you try to escape, you die."

Above, the ship turned. Their destination unknown. Korlue waited. For lightning, for Andrew, for the storm inside him to rise again.

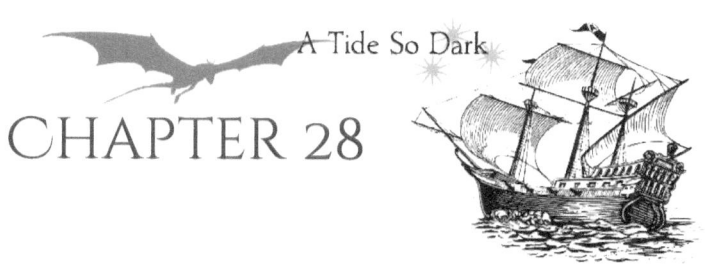

CHAPTER 28

T he door to the bookstore hung crooked on its hinges; the bell above it twisted and silent. Andrew stepped inside, Nideya right behind him, their boots crunching over glass. The air smelled of rain, blood, and scorched wood. Shelves had been torn apart. The counter splintered. The storm had passed—but something worse had come through.

As they went further in, the scent of blood lingered beneath the musk of old paper and damp wood.

Andrew swore under his breath.

They found him near the poetry section, curled on his side, with a shattered plate of beignets beside him. Powdered sugar dusted the floor like ash. His eyes were open.

Nideya dropped to her knees. Her fingers trembled, but she did not cry. She knew him well enough for tears, but there was no time for them. She reached out and gently closed his eyes.

"He loved this place," she whispered. "He kept tellin' me it felt like magic."

Andrew did not speak. He could not. The silence was unbearable. Panic set in. Then he saw it. Korlue's grounding necklace—blackened, cracked, lying in a pool of rainwater near the door. He picked it up with shaking hands. The metal was still warm.

"He's gone," he said. "Tempest took him."

Nideya's voice was quiet but certain. "I know. I saw it, in the ink. Not all of it. Just flashes. Tempest. The storm. Blood. Chains."

Andrew stood, fury rising like a tide. "Then help me find him."

"I will," she said, appearing beside him. "But I'm comin' with you."

"No," Andrew snapped. "It will be too dangerous. You will just get in my way."

"You need me," she reminded him. "And I'm not leaving him to die."

Andrew turned away, his fists clenched. "You do not understand what he means to me."

"I do," she said. "Because I saw it. In the ink. In the way you look at him when you think no one's watchin'."

He froze.

"I'm comin'," she repeated. "You'll need me."

Andrew looked at her, this strange, haunted girl with living ink in her veins and prophecy in her hands. She was trembling, but her eyes burned with resolve.

"You saw where he is?" he asked.

"Not exactly," she said. "But I can find him. I can paint the path."

Andrew slipped the broken necklace into his coat pocket. The storm had passed, but the real darkness was just beginning.

He turned to Nideya. "We will take Lucian back to his mother, then we will leave."

Together, they stepped out onto the wet streets of New Orleans, the sky still bruised with thunder, the ink in her blood already stirring.

Lucian's body was heavier than Andrew expected.

Not just the weight of a fourteen-year-old boy, but the weight of what had been done to him. Tempest had left him curled near the poetry shelf, blood soaked into the pages like ink. The storm had cleared, leaving behind silence and the smell of copper and burned, damp wood.

Nideya stood beside him, her ink-dark eyes unreadable, her face pale. She had asked to come with him to find Korlue, but first—they had to do this. They had to bring Lucian home.

Andrew wrapped the boy in the linen they kept for emergencies. It felt wrong. Too clinical. Too clean. Lucian had been messy and bright and loud. He deserved more than silence.

He lifted him carefully, cradling the body against his chest. His limbs hung limp, too long for Andrew's arms, too still for someone who had once danced between shelves like they were stepping stones.

Nideya moved out the door ahead of him.

The streets were quiet now, puddles reflecting the broken sky. The walk to the bakery was short, but it felt endless. People stared. No one spoke.

The scent of powdered sugar hit Andrew before the door even opened.

It clung to the air like a memory—warm, sweet, persistent. The kind of smell that made you think of laughter and sticky fingers, of mornings that began with soft dough and ended with powdered smiles. But today, it felt wrong. Too gentle for what they carried.

The bell above the door chimed, too bright, too cheerful.

Andrew bore the weight of Lucian's body in his arms, heavier now than it had been in the shop. He stepped forward, and the linen shifted. A glimpse of brown skin, a curl of hair still damp from the storm.

Eve was behind the counter when they arrived, her apron dusted with flour, a tray of beignets cooling beside her. She looked up; her smile already forming.

"Did he stay dry?" she asked. "Did he—"

Andrew stepped closer.

She saw the linen. The shape. The way Lucian's curls peeked out from the folds.

Her smile vanished.

"No," she said. "No, not my boy."

Andrew laid Lucian gently on the counter, beside the beignets. Powdered sugar drifted down, settling on the cloth like snow.

Eve did not move.

She stared at him. At Andrew. At Nideya.

Then she reached out slowly, as if she were afraid he would vanish if she touched him.

Her fingers brushed his cheek.

Lucian's face was peaceful. Too peaceful. His curls still damp, his lips parted as if mid-word. Eve touched his cheek, then his chest, then his hands. Her own hands were dusted with flour, and the white smeared across his skin like ash.

"He was just here," she said. "He was just laughing. He wanted to learn how to make the glaze—said he'd surprise Korlue."

Her voice broke.

Andrew swallowed hard. "We found him after the storm."

Eve's hands trembled. She pulled the cloth back further, revealing more of him. He was pale; there was no blood left in him. It had all soaked into his clothes, into the linen. Now he was just an empty shell of the boy they knew.

She did not scream.

She did not cry.

She just leaned down and kissed his forehead.

"I told him it wasn't safe to go out, but he was so insistent."

Andrew felt something twist in his chest. Guilt, maybe. Or grief. Or the knowledge that he had not gotten back to the shop fast enough, that he was not strong enough, anything enough.

Eve sat down behind the counter, cradling Lucian's body in her lap. The beignets cooled beside her, untouched.

"I'll keep the bakery open," she said softly. "I'll make them just the way he likes. Maybe he'll find his way back."

Nideya turned away, her face a mask of sorrow.

Andrew stayed.

Because sometimes, the only thing you could do was to bear witness.

CHAPTER 29

T he voyage to the Tidevault stretched across days that bled into one another. Their journey was long and brutal. The ship caved through waters thick with fog and memory, guided by Tempest's newfound knowledge of the approximate location.

The sea stilled.

Tempest stood at the prow of his ship, the wind quiet against his skin, the sky bruised with fading storm light. The Tidevault rose from the sea like a cathedral carved from grief. Its arches were slick with salt and time, its spires veined with coral and bone. The sea had remained still—unnaturally so—as if the water itself feared what was about to be remembered. The entrance pulsed faintly, like a wound that refused to heal.

They docked near the rocks surrounding the vault. Tempest stood at the threshold, the wind brushing his coat; the chalice pulsed slightly in his blood. This was it.

Behind him, Korlue was silent—chained, bruised, watching with eyes that burned. When Tempest was not playing with Korlue, he gave him the book on the chalice to read.

"You'll have to face your past when you enter," Korlue said, his voice hoarse. "It's not just a vault; it's a reckoning."

Tempest did not answer. He stepped forward. Inside, the chalice waited. But before he could reach it, the vault demanded its toll.

He removed his coat and tossed it onto the rocks before wading into the water. His whole body buzzed with anticipation as he pushed the doors open. At its center, a violet glow shimmered, lighting the echoing and vast interior. The Tideheart chalice was close. The walls breathed. And the past came for him.

She appeared first.

Aine.

Her name still tasted like longing. Her laughter echoed through the chamber, soft and cruel. She stood in the vision, radiant and unreachable, her hand resting in another man's. A man with eyes like storm light. Doyle. A man Tempest had hated for as long as he could remember. A sea king, like him.

But where Tempest was tide and blood, Doyle was current and shadows. Aine had chosen Doyle. Had borne his child. A daughter with eyes like her mother's and a foul mouth like her father.

Tempest had begged. Had raged. Had offered Aine the world. But she had turned away.

And so he took everything.

He killed Aine first—dragged her beneath the waves, whispered her name as he drowned her. Her final breath was a prayer for the man she loved, not for herself.

Years later, he found the daughter. She was barely grown. Contempt, not fear, was in her eyes as she looked at him. She reminded him too much of her mother—her eyes, her defiance.

He had her in every way conceivable, and still, she defied him. He killed her in front of the dragon. The boy screamed. Had tried to stop him. But he was weak then. Afraid.

The vault showed him everything. Her final breath. The silence that followed. The years of power, of conquest, of drowning himself in magic and flesh to forget the sounds of death.

Then—Korlue.

Bound. Defiant. Beautiful in his fury.

Tempest's breath caught. The ache was familiar. Different. Worse.

He stepped toward the chalice, trembling. The venom in his veins pulsed. The elemental magic surged, wild and sharp.

Korlue's voice echoed from the entrance. "You know what it wants. You can't take its power without giving something precious."

Tempest closed his eyes and searched for the memories that were most precious to him. "I give her," he whispered. "Aine. The woman I loved. The one I destroyed."

The chalice pulsed.

"I give her daughter," he said, his voice cracking. "The child I stole from the sea."

The vault trembled.

"And I give my love of him," Tempest said, barely breathing. "Korlue. The only thing I've wanted since."

The chalice accepted the offerings. He picked up the cup; it was filled with the purest water. He placed his lips on the cup and swallowed. Light surged through him—cold and cleansing. His body shuddered as the rot was stripped away, the hunger silenced, the elemental magic sharpened to its purest edge. He gasped, restored. Reborn.

But something inside him had died, and the scar on his throat remained. A reminder of his sacrifice.

He emerged from the vault changed. Stronger. Colder. The chalice in hand.

Korlue looked up at him, chained and silent. "You used me," he said after a moment.

Tempest knelt beside him, brushing damp hair from his face. "I loved you. That's why it worked."

Korlue turned away. "Then it wasn't love."

Tempest did not argue. He stood calling out to his men. "Lock him back up. We return to the hideout."

One crewman hesitated. "Why bring him with us?"

Tempest's voice was quiet. "Because he's bait."

"Why?" Korlue asked, panicked.

Tempest looked back, eyes gleaming. "Because he'll come for you. Your dragon. And when he does, I'll have everything I need."

Korlue did not speak. He let himself be dragged back to the ship; the chalice was locked below deck; the ocean rose around them like a grave.

Tempest looked out at the sea, the chalice pulsing beneath his feet. Soon, his revenge will be complete.

CHAPTER 30

T he rented boat groaned against the dock ropes, its hull weathered and salt-stained. Andrew stood at the bow, scanning the horizon as the sun dipped low, casting the sea in bruised gold. Nideya sat beside him, her sketchbook open, fingers stained with ink that shimmered faintly in the fading light. It had been a long time since he had sailed. The memory of his last voyage was bittersweet.

Andrew leaned against the railing, still searching the horizon with eyes that had not truly rested in days. The salt air stung his throat, but it was the silence that gnawed at him—the absence of Korlue's voice, the memory of his grounding necklace lying broken on the floor. Their last interaction had been in anger. Andrew cursed himself for having chased Nideya off. Korlue would still be with him had he not.

Beside him, Nideya sketched quietly. Her hair clung to her cheeks, damp from sea spray and sweat. She had spoken little since the last port. He had needed to keep his fire fueled, so he had fed on the local vagrants.

They had stopped at seven ports already. Each had yielded nothing—no sight of the Pale Emperor, no whispers of Tempest's crew. Just blank stares and shrugged shoulders. The trail was growing cold.

Andrew's jaw was tight. His knuckles white on the railing. "He is out there," he muttered. "I know he is."

Nideya did not answer. Her ink had been restless for days, twitching beneath her skin, whispering in her dreams. He could hear her talking in her sleep. But it had not shown her anything clear—just fragments. Storms. Chains. A chalice pulsing in the dark.

Andrew's hope was fraying.

Until they reached the eighth port.

It was a quiet port town tucked into a crescent of rocky shore; the buildings faded and leaning, the people wary. Something had happened there; he could feel it in the way they looked at the sea, like it owed them something it had stolen.

A shopkeeper finally spoke.

"My wife," he said, his voice low. "She vanished two nights ago. I saw the ship. White sails. Pale hull. Looked like it was carved from bone."

Andrew's heart pounded. "Did you hear where they were going?"

The man hesitated. "One of the crew said something about a hidden cove. A place that don't show on maps. They called it the Hollow."

They returned to the boat in silence. But the moment they stepped aboard, Nideya collapsed to her knees, her eyes wide and unfocused. The ink surged from her skin, spilling across

183

the deck in frantic strokes. Andrew knelt beside her, gripping her shoulders.

"Nideya—"

She did not hear him.

Her hand moved as if it were not hers, painting with speed and precision. The image took shape: jagged cliffs, a black sea, a hidden inlet shrouded by mist, and three stars above. And in the foreground—Korlue.

He was lying on the ground. Motionless. His hair was damp with seawater. His eyes closed.

And behind him, smiling—Tempest.

The smile was wrong. Too calm. Too certain.

Andrew stared at the painting, his breath caught in his throat. The ink shimmered, alive and pulsing, as if the vision itself was bleeding.

"He's there," Nideya whispered, her voice raw. "They're both there. He's already used the chalice."

Andrew touched the image of Korlue, his fingers trembling. "Is he alive?"

"I don't know," she said.

Andrew stood, fury rising like a tide. "Then we go now."

Nideya looked up at him, her eyes dark and ancient. "We'll need more than rage."

Andrew did not answer. He turned toward the helm, the painting still wet behind him, the sea rising around them like a warning.

CHAPTER 31

His screams echoed throughout the cavern, the pain seemingly unending as Jonas ripped them from his sore, tired throat. Korlue sobbed uncontrollably, begging for it all to end. Then he blacked out, unable to bear the torment any longer.

The stone floor was slick with seawater, the tide creeping in through cracks. Korlue lay curled against the wall, his body aching in places he had not known could ache. Jonas had left him again—bored, perhaps, or simply done for the day. Jonas never lingered once the thrill faded. He preferred silence after violence, like a collector discarding a broken artifact.

Korlue scoffed at the memory of wanting more adventure, more excitement in his life. Now he longed for the quiet and the sameness of the days before.

His wrists throbbed where the shackles had bitten deep. At least his tormentor was gone for now—after the bruises, after the blood, after the whispered mockeries that no longer stung. Korlue's lightning was gone—dampened by the necklace Jonas had fastened around his throat, a cruel mockery of the one Andrew had once given him. That one had been a promise. This one was a leash.

There was no love left in Jonas, only possession. Only power. Only vengeance.

He closed his eyes. And memory came unbidden. Not the pain. Not the cell. But the first time Andrew had found him.

It was at a local bookstore. Korlue had been a Host then. A fancy, customizable courtesan. A beautiful thing kept behind velvet curtains, trained to smile and bleed on command. His body had been currency. His silence, a commodity. He had learned how to survive by becoming what others wanted—never what he wanted.

Until Andrew.

He had not come to buy him. He had only wanted to talk. Korlue remembered the way Andrew had looked at him—not with hunger, not with pity, but with confusion. He had been attracted to Korlue and did not know what to do with that.

They had a rocky start. Andrew had nearly killed Korlue by accident, but he had found him again years later and offered Korlue a way out. They had built Bound to Please together. Brick by brick. Shelf by shelf. It had been their sanctuary. Their rebellion. A place where stories mattered more than scars. Where Korlue could be more than beautiful. Where Andrew could be more than dangerous.

Andrew never flinched. Not when Korlue woke up screaming after what Dorjan had done to him. Not when Korlue told him everything.

Andrew feared nothing... except losing him.

And now, in this cell carved from salt and silence, Korlue felt the fear echoing in his own chest. Not for himself. For his mate. He thought of the way Andrew carried guilt like armor, how he never asked for forgiveness because he did not believe he deserved it.

Korlue understood now.

Andrew's past was not just dangerous. It was a shadow that followed him. And Korlue had stepped into it willingly. But he did not regret it. If he ever saw him again—if Nideya's ink still whispered true, if the sea had not swallowed them both—then they would talk. Not about escape. Not about revenge. About safety. About truth. And how to protect each other from the ghosts that still lingered. If Andrew chose truth, Korlue would stay.

Even broken. Even afraid.

Because love, once given freely, does not vanish. It changes shape. It adapts. And it survives... just like him.

CHAPTER 32

T he cliffs loomed like broken teeth against the sky, jagged and slick with mist. The inlet was quiet, too quiet, the water unnaturally still. Andrew guided the boat into the cove, his jaw clenched, his eyes fixed on the cave mouth carved into the rock like a wound. He hated caves; they brought back so many terrible memories.

Nideya stood beside him, her ink-stained fingers trembling. "You stay here," he said, his voice low. "Hidden."

She did not argue. She simply nodded, her eyes dark with knowing.

Andrew stepped onto the shore, the sand crunching beneath his boots. The cave swallowed him whole. Inside, the air was thick with the familiar smell of salt and rot. He swore the walls pulsed faintly, as if the stone itself remembered pain. Tempest's men waited in the shadows—silent, armed, loyal. Andrew did not hesitate.

He moved like fire.

The first fell with his own blade to the throat. The second with a burst of flame that lit the cavern in green. A third tried to run. He did not make it far. None of them did. There was a Vanita that stood proud against him, sending his Nyxkin out to stop Andrew, but even with his shadow-eating monsters, the Vanita was no match for him. Andrew lit them all on fire without a second thought.

He stepped over the bodies of Tempest's men, his boots echoing against the stone. The air reeked of magic—wet, metallic, and ancient. The sounds of fighting died out, replaced by the sound of skin smacking skin in rapid succession, and loud grunts and groans.

He found them in the heart of the Hollow.

Andrew froze.

Tempest had Korlue bent over in front of him, one hand pressed to his back as he fucked him from behind. He was draining the life from him in slow, deliberate pulses. Korlue's body was limp; his already pale skin looked translucent. What looked like a power-dampening collar locked around his throat. He had a vacant look in his now pale-blue eyes. His lips moved faintly, but no sound came.

Tempest looked up, then smiled. "You're late." He slapped Korlue's ass as he continued to thrust in and out of him at a harsh pace. "I got bored—and hungry," he grinned devilishly.

Andrew stepped forward, his fury rising like a tsunami. "Let him go," he growled.

Tempest tilted his head. "You came for love. How sweet. Let's see if it's enough." He tossed Korlue aside like a broken doll, then put away his cock.

Korlue hit the stone with a sickening thud.

Andrew did not wait. With a stolen sword in hand, he lunged.

Tempest met him with a wall of water, crashing against Andrew's body and slamming him into the cave wall. Andrew rolled, coughing, flames already licking at his fingertips. He threw a burst of fire that seared across Tempest's shoulder, but the former sea king twisted, absorbing the heat into mist that hissed and vanished.

"You think your rage makes you strong?" Tempest sneered. "I've killed real warriors for less."

Andrew charged again, blade drawn, slicing through the air. Tempest blocked with a whip of water, the strike sending sparks into the dark. They collided—flesh, magic, fury—each blow echoing centuries of grief.

Tempest struck with blood magic, trying to seize Andrew's veins, to twist his body against itself. Andrew roared, fire erupting from his chest, burning through the spell. He slammed Tempest into an altar, an ornate cup rattling beside them.

"I am not the boy you abused so long ago," Andrew growled.

"Perhaps not, but I reckon he's still in there somewhere," Tempest grinned, struggling against him.

Andrew's eyes burned. "I will kill you."

Tempest laughed as he surged forward, water crashing around him. He was fast—inhumanly fast—but Andrew was relentless. Despite how tired he was, he fought like a man with nothing left to lose.

They grappled, their power flaring. Tempest tried to drown him. Andrew set the cave alight, feeling the drain of his life force from where Tempest held on to him. He broke free and put distance between them before he shifted into his bestial form. Bones cracked and skin split as his wolf broke free.

"Well, that's different," Tempest said in surprise. "But it won't save you."

When Tempest raised his hand to strike, Andrew lunged forward with greater speed than he had before and knocked Tempest off his feet. They rolled around on the cave floor with Andrew snapping at Tempest's face and whatever he could get to.

Andrew felt Tempest's weight shift as he had transformed into his demonic state for added strength. His horns curved around his ears, and his body thickened with added muscle.

Tempest tossed Andrew into the nearest wall, rock cracking and crumbling with the force of the throw. Andrew slid down the wall, limp, but not out of the fight. He staggered to his feet, then howled before charging at Tempest again.

Tempest caught him mid-leap, and Andrew could feel the life draining from him again as they continued their brutal fight, slamming each other into the cave walls and the ground.

Andrew slashed at Tempest with his claws before he hurled his body into him. Tempest took hold of him, and again, Andrew felt his life slowly ebbing away. But when he was about to lose consciousness, he caught Tempest by the throat.

He brought him down, clamping his jaws tighter. His teeth sank deeper into his flesh until he hit bone. There was a crunch and tearing as skin and muscle pulled away, blood spilling in large fountain-like bursts as Tempest clawed, kicked, and gurgled until Andrew tore his head from his body.

The light in Tempest's eyes flickered. The surrounding water stilled.

Andrew shook his head, sending globs of blood and ichor in all directions, then shifted back, then set the corpse on fire. He would make sure there was nothing left of the monster. Once he was satisfied, he dropped to his knees beside Korlue.

"Kory," he whispered. "Please."

No response.

He touched his face. Cold.

He howled—raw, broken; the sound echoing through the cave like a curse. He begged and cried, pressing his forehead to Korlue's chest and whispering prayers he had not spoken in centuries.

Then he scrambled towards the chalice. It pulsed in his hands, beautiful and cruel. He tried to use it. Tried to pour its power into Korlue's body.

Nothing. It only worked on the living, he surmised. He took hold of Korlue's limp hand and sobbed. There was nothing he could do now. He was immortal. He knew he would outlive Korlue, but he had hoped it would not be this soon.

Andrew collapsed beside him, trembling. "Please," he whispered in tears. "Please, someone..."

And then—light. Soft and sacred.

She appeared in the glow; he could not make out much of her form. But her voice was wind and water, her eyes older than stars. He remembered her.

"You ask for life," she said. "But life demands a price."

Andrew did not hesitate. "Take it. My life for his."

She tilted her head. "Your immortality. The chalice. All of it."

He nodded. "Take them; they mean nothing without my love. Just bring him back."

She reached out and touched his chest.

The chalice disappeared. The magic of his immortality left him—he felt it go, like breath, like blood. He saw a light travel from him into Korlue's lifeless form.

And then—Korlue gasped.

His eyes fluttered open. His body shuddered. He looked up at Andrew, confused, afraid—and then he saw him.

They embraced.

No words. Just arms around each other, tears mixing with seawater, silence thick with love.

Outside, Nideya waited on the boat.

When they emerged naked and wrapped in blankets, she ran to them, relief on her face. She did not ask what had happened. She did not need to.

The three of them boarded the boat. And together, they returned to New Orleans. Home.

EPILOGUE

T he bookstore was still scarred.

Sunlight filtered through the cracked windows, catching on dust motes and the jagged edges of broken shelves. The scent of lemon oil and old paper hung in the air, mingling with the faint trace of rain. The sign above the door swayed slightly in the breeze, its letters faded but defiant.

Korlue sat in the armchair near the counter, wrapped in a soft wool blanket, his body still recovering from the damage Jonas had done. His lightning had returned, faint and flickering beneath his skin, but the dampener necklace had left a mark— one that would not fade easily.

Andrew knelt beside him, one hand resting on Korlue's knee, the other gently brushing a strand of hair from his face. "You are safe now," he said. "Dorjan is gone, and Tempest is dead. There is no one left to take you from me."

Korlue's eyes searched his face. "You can't promise that."

Andrew's voice did not waver. "I can. Because I will burn the world down before I let it happen again."

Korlue smiled, weak but real. "I believe that."

They sat in silence for a while, the kind that only came after surviving something unspeakable. Korlue was not yet ready to talk about what all that had happened to him; he still had trouble sleeping because of the trauma, but he knew Andrew would always be there when he needed him. He barely left his side as it was.

Though he was not ready to discuss all that Jonas had done to him, Korlue asked what had happened while he was unconscious.

"You died, Kory," Andrew answered reluctantly. "I killed Tempest, but I arrived too late to save you."

Korlue furrowed his brows. "Then how am I still here? Did you use the chalice?"

Again, Andrew hesitated before answering. "No, the chalice only works on the living, I think. I gave it and my immortality to the goddess that saved me."

Korlue was silent now. He was not sure what to say in response.

Before he could speak again, Andrew silenced him. "It is all right. I can still heal my wounds quickly. I am still me, and I look forward to eventually growing old with you now."

Andrew's gentle smile broke Korlue. They kissed and embraced, but spoke no more of it.

Outside, Nideya swept the front steps, her ink-stained fingers moving with quiet purpose. Korlue admired her courage. She had stood up to Andrew when he was distraught and angry, demanding to accompany him on his rescue mission. Had it not been for her and her painting, they might never have found him.

The next morning, the shop came alive again.

Andrew and Nideya worked side by side, hammering shelves back into place, re-shelving books that had been scattered like fallen leaves. Korlue supervised from his chair, offering quiet suggestions, his voice steadier now. He refused to rest completely—he needed to see the store whole again. Needed to see them whole again.

They mourned Lucian together. His name was spoken softly, reverently. A plate of beignets was left on the repaired counter, dusted with powdered sugar, untouched. Korlue lit a candle beside them. Andrew did not speak; he just stood with his hand on Korlue's shoulder, eyes closed.

"He should've been here," Korlue whispered.

"He is," Andrew said. "In every book we shelve. Every morning we wake up and choose to keep going."

Korlue nodded and said a silent prayer for his lost friend.

Later, as the sun dipped low, Korlue and Andrew sat together in the back room, the air warm with candlelight and the scent of old paper.

"She shouldn't be alone," Korlue said, watching Nideya through the doorway as she sorted books with quiet focus. "She doesn't have anywhere to go."

Andrew nodded. "She is strong."

"She's still a child."

Andrew was quiet for a moment. "If she wants to stay, she earns her keep. No excuses."

Korlue smiled. "You've gone soft."

"I am practical."

They called Nideya back. She stood in the doorway, ink still staining her fingers, her eyes wide and waiting.

Andrew crossed his arms. "You want to stay?"

She nodded.

"Then you help. You work. You do not vanish when things get hard."

"I won't," she said. "I want to be here." She stepped forward and held out her sketchbook. "I finished something," she admitted. "It's not... bad."

Korlue took it gently. Andrew leaned in.

The drawing was soft-warm tones, gentle lines. It showed the three of them in the store. Andrew was behind the counter, Korlue was reading in his chair, and she was painting in the corner. The light in the image was golden. Peaceful.

Andrew stared at it for a long time.

Korlue's breath caught. "It's beautiful."

Nideya smiled. "It's the future. Maybe."

Korlue reached out and touched her hand. "It's a beginning."

That night, they shared dinner at the table—bread, soup, and quiet laughter. Nideya told stories about the ink's moods. Andrew fussed at Korlue about his stubborn refusal to rest. Korlue watched them both, heart aching with something that felt like joy.

Outside, the wind stirred. And inside, for the first time in a long while, the world felt quiet.

OTHER WORKS BY
EMBER DRAKE

 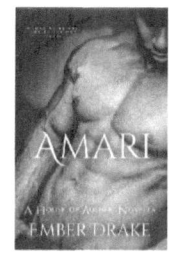 

About the Author

Ember Drake is an American author from Columbia, South Carolina. She has been writing since the age of ten and has aspired to be a published author ever since. Ember has always had a love of dragons and wolves. As a joke, she was told that all she needed was to put them together and then she would be happy. This resulted in the creation of Raesh, who was modeled after her favorite former Power Ranger, Johnny Yong Bosch. Roland/Zaven was modeled after her favorite actor, Matt Ryan.

She had been working on the House of Ausher series since the age of seventeen. It was just three short stories that only included vampires and werewolves, both of which she is a huge fan of. The series evolved from terrible Backstreet Boys fan fiction about three brothers to what it is today.

Visit <u>EmberDrakeAuthor.com</u> for news and updates!